KAISHI

The Beginning

NINJANS 1

Dave Kwan

DISCLAIMER

Book Cover Credit: Artwork by Daniel - Adobe Stock

File#: 268140154 JPEG 4200 x 2800px

ISBN:
ISBN-13:9781777310837

To my lovely wife, Merle,
who encouraged me to write.

CHAPTER ONE

The Ninja of Iga Mountain

The early mountain mist lifts as the sun rises on the horizon. The rays of light fall across the lone shadowy figure to reveal a seasoned Ninja Master, his long whispy white beard in contrast to his black outfit. The aged Ninja Master looks out over the line of young lads dressed in Ninja white, each with a bow and quiver of black arrows. The man raises his arm in the air. The young men quickly fix arrow to bow and pull back the bowstring - and hold. Most keep a steady hand, while only a few shake and wobble as they aim. One hundred feet in front of them are weathered chipped wooden posts. The old Ninja Master watches keenly how the lads stand and position their arrows — The old man drops his arm and all the young men shoot their arrows - WHOOSH! A stream of black arrows fly through the air to strike each post, each arrow tip sinks in, adding yet another hole in the perforated surface. Each and every lad hit their target. All the lads with smiles of accomplishment look over at their Teacher. The old man with twinkling eyes, nods his approval. Further away on an upper elevation, the Ninja Clan Leaders watch the training exercise with contented smiles.

The high elevation and rugged terrain of the Iga Mountains is where the Ninja Clans have built their villages. Each Clan has its own village of wooden houses, neatly and efficiently laid out to optimize any available land for their vegetables, chickens and goats. The family dwellings are constructed entirely of wood precisely cut, trimmed and fitted together like a giant jigsaw. The Japanese carpenters do not use metal nails like their counterparts in Europe and America, the Japanese carpenters cut, shape and join the wooden parts to fit and lock together. The construction of a traditional Japanese wood house is both ingenious and practical.

The Ninja Clan villagers are busy with daily life. The women prepare the food, cook meals and wash clothes; while the men care for livestock, mend fences, till the soil, and make wood items. Both young and old, both men and women, help plant and harvest rice from the water paddies. The older children tend the goats, feed the chickens, and do necessary errands. The younger children run, play and laugh, as children do everywhere. The mountain villagers are cheerful and cordial, and greet each other with traditional bows of respect.

Young lads, trainees all dressed in white, stand in the centre of a large semi-circle. Around them various Ninja Instructors display their weapon specialty. The young men are fascinated. At one end, an Instructor twirls a metal chain dart and flings it to impale a small target. Nearby, a Ninja Master deftly handles and spins two razor sharp Kusarigama - Sickles. To the left, another Instructor throws Shuriken with deadly accuracy - the pointed metal stars sink deep into targets. To the right at the opposite end, a Ninja Master swiftly runs, jumps and summersaults to land on top a large wooden post. The faces of the trainees are full of awe and wonder at seeing such skills.

A middle-aged man, Katsu, the Sword Master, approaches the group of young men. Katsu is lean and muscular and holds a Katana sword. All the trainees stand attentive and silent. Katsu looks intently at the young men to make eye contact and remarks, "Each of you will learn the Ninja weapons and fighting techniques. When you have mastered them and proved your skill - you will join our Ninja ranks." The Sword Master lifts his hand and points, "For now, you begin with the humble staff." The group of trainees walk over and stand before the Staff Master, an elderly man holding a long smooth staff. The old man gestures to a pile of poles on the ground. All the young trainees grab a pole and reassemble ready for instruction. The aged Staff Master strides over to three trainees at the front and gives each a knife. The man walks 20 yards away, then turns and motions, "You three - attack me with your knives." The three trainees look at each other, then quickly move out. One lad lunges with his blade, the other slashes wildly with his knife, and the third lad throws his weapon. The trainees watch as the old Instructor spins the staff to block the thrown knife, shoot out the pole to buckle the lunging attacker, and twirls the staff to knock the blade out of the slasher's hand. The trainees are in awe! One excited young recruit pipes up, "Master, when will you teach us to fight like this?" The Staff Master looks at the trainees, grips the staff with both hands and replies, "You must first learn how to hold the staff, then after much practice, when you are ready, I will teach you such techniques, (He pauses), for now, spread out and find a space to swing your staff without hitting others." The eager recruits find positions, and the Staff Master begins instruction on proper stance, balance, arm position and hand grip. The elderly Instructor leads the recruits through the basics - how to hold, raise, block, lower, extend and swing the staff. Each trainee is diligent and pays close attention.

Off to the side, high up in the thick brush, two Imperial Japanese soldiers hide as they spy out the Ninja villages. One soldier uses a charcoal pencil to sketch out the Ninja villages, the buildings and layout. When finished, the soldier rolls up the parchment and slides the drawing into a leather cylinder case. The two Imperial soldiers quietly sneak away undetected by the Ninja below.

Nestled among the neat rows of homes lays the Sword Master's family dwelling. Aiko is his kind and gentle wife, who kneels in the kitchen beside a low table and uses a ladle to scoop vegetable soup from a pot to pour into ceramic bowls on the table. Aiko's Japanese kimono is simple yet elegant. An intricate ivory comb decorates her pinned up hair. Her make up is modest since her features are refined and beautiful, her smile is pleasant and sweet. Katsu's two young children, his son Takeshi (10) and daughter Rei (8), sit still and respectful on cushions beside the table.

Footsteps sound on the lacquered wood floor announcing the Sword Master has entered his home. Katsu stands in the home's open area, his bearing exudes noble character. Aiko, Takeshi and Rei turn and give the traditional bow of respect to their father, who is head of the household and also a Ninja Leader. Katsu nods to his wife and children, then enters a side room only to emerge moments later dressed in his comfortable home attire. He comes and sits cross-legged on a cushion beside the table. Katsu gives a warm smile to Aiko, Takeshi and Rei - then he reaches out to clasp and bring close the inviting bowl of soup. Now that the husband and father has begun to eat, Aiko and the children take their soup bowls to enjoy the savoury meal. The family members pick greens, bean sprouts and shredded cabbage from small bowls on the table to add to their soup. The family of four eat in quiet contentment.

It is late afternoon when young Takeshi makes his way to the Swordsmith Shed where his father, Katsu, is working on a new sword. As the young lad approaches and peers into the shadowy interior, he sees his dad illuminated in a golden light from the glowing coals of the forge. Takeshi enters the structure and comes beside his dad, who is intently focused on working the bellows which makes the liquid metal bubble in the cauldron. Satisfied, Katsu uses long metal tongs to grab the vessel of molten metal and carry it over to a mould nearby. Takeshi's young eyes watch as his dad tilts the tongs to pour the molten metal into the empty mould. The golden liquid metal cascades from the cauldron and runs throughout the mould to cover and slowly fill the cavity. Soon, the liquid metal rises and reaches the brim of the mould. Katsu stops pouring and sets the tongs and cauldron aside. Katsu notices Takeshi's fascination. The father looks at his son and remarks, "You are old enough now to learn the art of Japanese sword making. I will teach you the materials to use and the proper mixture, how to heat the metal and work the steel. You will learn to grind, hone and polish the blade to become a Ninja sword." Takeshi eyes light up and he smiles at his father and bows, "Father, I will study hard and be your best pupil!" Katsu grins at Takeshi's childlike enthusiasm and demeanour, "My son, knowing how to use a sword is good. But knowing how to make your own sword is even better!" The father reaches out to playfully mess Takeshi's hair, "From this day, you will be my assistant in making the swords!" Takeshi with excited eyes and fetching smile, bows low, "Thank you father! I am greatly honoured." Katsu turns his attention to the hardened newly-shaped form, and grabs the red hot steel with tongs and carries it over to the blacksmith anvil. There, Katsu repeatedly pounds the red hot steel with a metal hammer, and sparks fly at each strike of the mallet. The man hits the metal, then dunks it into a vat of water; this is repeated many times. Takeshi watches as his dad bends and shapes the metal into a thick curved flat bar - the noticeable rough outline of a curved Katana sword. Katsu lifts up the metal form to examine if it's straight, properly curved, and of the correct thickness. Next, he places the flat bar into the burning coals of the forge - the metal bar changes from black to red hot steel - then Katsu swiftly moves it to the anvil where he pounds and strikes the glowing hot metal to form the blade and point of the sword. Takeshi observes his father perspire greatly as he quickly works between the glowing coals of the forge and the hard labour of striking and shaping the blade. Finally, Katsu holds aloft the fashioned metal that now clearly represents a Katana blade. Takeshi has been quiet throughout his father's intense labour. The father glances at his boy and comments, "The blade has the proper shape, now I will grind and sharpen the steel into a proper sword." Takeshi nods his young head and smiles wide. The lad looks up at the ceiling at the far side of the Swordsmith Shed. Beautiful finished swords hang from the rafters, each sword depicts skilled craftsmanship and wonderful design in its handle and scabbard. As Katsu continues to grind and perfect the newly formed blade, Takeshi's face is full of awe and excitement.

CHAPTER TWO
The Warlord Attacks

The Warlord sits as a Monarch on his gold throne. Court Officials, Dignitaries, Military Commanders, Castle Guards, and household servants are before him. The Warlord's Concubines sit off to a distance at the side. The Castle interior is richly decorated with lavish tapestries, carved stone statues, exquisite jade art, guilded furniture, and large paintings depicting Japanese life. At the opposite end of the Throne Chamber are two massive iron doors embellished with motifs and engravings of the Warlord's symbol, a roaring tiger with claws extended. Four Guards stand sentry at the large metal doors.

Clang! Clang! The heads and eyes of everyone within the Castle Chamber turn toward the two doors. The Sentries look at the Warlord for his instruction. With a flick of his hand, the ruler motions the Guards to open the doors to grant admission. As the giant doors swing open, the two Imperial soldiers that spied on the Ninja villages stand alert and at attention - waiting to be be summoned forward. These two soldiers had learned that in the past, when someone entered the Warlord's Chamber without his approval - it cost them their lives. The duo look expectantly at the Warlord, who rises from his Throne Chair to stand and wave them forward. The assembled Courtiers, Commanders, Nobility and servants quickly part to make way. The two spies hasten to the steps of the Throne and swiftly bow - one soldier holds out his hand with the leather cylinder. A nearby Military Commander clasps the cylinder, ascends up the steps, bows and extends the cylinder to the Ruler. Upon the Warlord taking the object, the Commander backs down the steps with his eyes lowered. He immediately positions himself with the other Generals. The Warlord opens the cylinder and takes out the scroll which he unrolls to his delight: SKETCH OF THE NINJA VILLAGES. The Warlord's eyes run across the drawing showing the terrain, layout and buildings. The Warlord holds the scroll high in the air, and he looks at his Military Leaders, "Commanders, ready your troops! We march to the Iga Mountains to ATTACK!" The Commanders immediately acknowledge with a bow, abruptly pivot and quickly hasten away. The entire assembly becomes abuzz as people disperse. Officials, Regional Dignitaries and attendants scurry off in all directions. A squad of Castle Guards assemble at the base of the Throne. The Warlord stands tall and proud as he holds the scroll with a firm grip - he stares ahead with fiery eyes.

Thousands of Imperial soldiers dressed for battle, stand alert and ready with their shields, spears, bows and swords. The foot soldiers amassed in columns hold position. Battalion Banners fly in the wind. Military Commanders sit mounted on horses. The adrenaline flows through both man and animal. Suddenly, the big iron gates of the Castle creak open - and out rides the Warlord on his white stallion, dressed in his gold battle armour. Royal Guards ride behind and carry the Ruler's Ensign of a Gold Tiger against an indigo background. The Commanders and troops snap to attention. The Warlord rides up to his top Commander, who swiftly remarks, "Your troops are ready my Lord!" The Ruler looks into his eyes and orders, "March until we reach the mountains. Our surprise attack will wipe out the Ninja Clans. They have become too strong and must be destroyed!" The Commander assures his Monarch, "Your army will overpower them. Victory will be yours!" Immediately, the top Commander rides to the other Generals. He signals and the Commanders move out their troops. The long column of soldiers stretch from the Warlord's Castle far into the distance.

The Warlord on his white horse, rides with his Generals to lead the Army. The Ruler's Gold Tiger Ensign flaps majestic in the breeze. The long column of soldiers march their way past farms, fields, villages and roadside Inns. The Japanese peasants and villagers bow low as the Warlord and his army pass by. A middle-aged farmer and his teenage son stop their labour as the Military mass approach their crop field. The father and son bow low, the son lifts his eyes ever-so-slightly to watch the soldiers and Banners go by. The farmer whispers a rebuke to his son, "Lower your gaze before they notice and gouge out your eyes!" The boy becomes alarmed and swiftly lowers his gaze to the ground. His father's face shows great relief. Time grows as the thousands of troops march past their field. The son whispers, "Father, my back hurts!" The farmer warns, "Stay bowed or we loose our lives! The soldiers will put us to their sword for dishonouring the Warlord and his Banner." The son gently nods his head, clenches his fists and holds steady. Soon, the soldiers of the Rearguard march by and move further down the road. The father and son raise themselves up. The farmer gives his son an intense look and remarks, "The army march in the direction of the Iga Mountains. We must secretly run ahead and warm the Ninja that live there!" The father puts his arm on the lad's shoulder. The son looks into his father's face and nods. The two quickly sprint across their crop field to the trees beyond.

Some time later...

The father and son run through the forest, across grassy meadows, over tilled fields, and along rural pathways used by peasants. The man and boy hasten with all their might, at one point, the lad grabs his stomach - cramps! The father looks back to see his son bent over with grimaced face, he runs to the lad's side. The boy looks up at his father, "I have to stop. My stomach hurts." The farmer coaxes the lad to lay flat on his back on the ground. With the son stretched out, the father kneads and massages the lad's stomach and lower sides. The lad's face shows relief, "The cramps are gone, I feel better." His father smiles, "Your stomach muscles are loosened up, we can move now." The man helps his son off the ground and turns to the tree grove, he puts his hand on the boy's shoulder, and speaks encouragement, "The mountains are not far. The Warlord's army is large and marches slow. We must hurry!" The son nods and both dash off to the grove of trees in the distance.

The Ninja Clan leaders are in the large wood building in the village centre. Katsu and the other Ninja Clan leaders are gathered around the farmer and his teenage son. Both stand sweaty and tired from the exhausting run, they breathe heavy to catch their breath. Hotaka, the top Ninja leader, a robust man with thick black hair and sideburns, offers them both a cup of water and points to a long wooden bench, "Sit, rest, drink some water." The farmer and lad take the wooden cups and gulp the water to quench their thirst. Hotaka looks at the farmer and enquires, "How many were they?" The farmer's eyes get wide and he waves his hand excitedly, "We saw thousands! A large army of Imperial soldiers marching toward the mountains." Kenta, a Ninja

Clan leader with salt and pepper hair tied in a ponytail, positions beside Hotaka to advise, "We must prepare our people! Anyone that can fight." Hotaka looks at the farmer and son, then glances at the other Ninja Clan leaders. He directs his gaze to Masa, an older man with a face full of wisdom and understanding, "How many Ninja do we have?" Masa ponders a second then replies, "Four thousand strong!" The Ninja Clan leaders look at each other. Katsu breaks the silence, "So few against so many! We need to assemble our warriors - and send our women and children away." His words strike home in the hearts of the other leaders and they nod agreement. Hotaka paces a bit then turns toward his fellow Ninja and instructs, "The four thousand will defend our villages - our best scouts will lead the women and children to safety through the secret tunnel." All the Clan leaders nod with determined expressions. Hotaka walks over to a table and motions the other leaders to gather around. He opens a long leather cylinder case and pulls out a large rolled up parchment. Hotaka sets the case aside and unrolls the big map and lays it on the table. All the Ninja Clan leaders huddle and begin to plan their defence.

A day has passed…

Regiments of Imperial soldiers hide in strategic positions across the mountain terrain. The Warlord's troops surround the three Ninja villages. The settlements look sleepy and peaceful. A Commander waves his arm and an archer pulls back a large bow and shoots a Whistle Arrow high into the sky. A loud shrill fills the air - the signal to ATTACK! Thousands of soldiers pour down upon the Ninja villages, the Warlord's troops attack from the North, South, East and West. As the Imperial troops get near - suddenly, hundreds of black clad Ninja appear for battle. Volleys of black arrows and explosive projectiles strike and kill the Warlord's troops. The Ninja warriors with gleaming steel swords run directly at the advancing army. The small force and large army collide. Arrows fly, swords slice, axes chop, Shuriken stars strike deep - it's a brutal bloody battle! The Ninja fight off the first wave, but being vastly outnumbered, the battle cost the Ninja a great number of warriors. The Ninja look around to see thousands of Imperial soldiers still coming. Hotaka, Masa, Kenta and Katsu signal their warriors to fall back. The Ninja fight valiantly to defend their people and homes. As the fighting becomes more intense, Hotaka waves Katsu over, "Go with our Scouts and lead our women and children to safety!" Katsu lifts his sword, "I will fight beside you as the

Ninja brothers we are." Hotaka smiles at his old friend, "No one knows our Ninja sword making like you. I want you to escape and keep our Ninja ways alive." Katsu looks about at the onslaught of soldiers racing toward them, he looks his dear friend in the eye. Hotaka pushes Katsu in the direction of the mountainside behind them, "Go old friend! Lead our people to safety and take our Ninja secrets with you." Katsu watches as his friend Hotaka turns and runs toward the hordes of armed soldiers. Soon, Hotaka is in the thick of battle surrounded by Imperial troops. Katsu waves to a couple of Ninja close by, and together they race up the mountainside. A Commander and garrison of soldiers chase after Katsu and his Ninja companions. Fleeing up the winding pathway that rises higher and higher, Katsu and the Ninja see the women and children huddled in seclusion. A few Ninja have accompanied them for safety. The group get up from their concealment - relieved to see Katsu and his fellow Ninja. Katsu looks at the group, "We must quickly flee. The Warlord's soldiers are closing in." Just as he finishes his words, down the mountainside, the Commander and his troops climb toward them. The Ninja that followed Katsu look at him, then raise their Katana swords and race to intercept the attackers - sacrificing their lives to buy time for the others. Katsu and the few remaining Ninja quickly guide the women and children up the mountain path to the secret tunnel that's camouflaged by bushes. Katsu stands at the tunnel entrance and oversees as the people hasten into the dark. A couple Ninja light torches to illuminate the tunnel for the people to move forward. Soon, all the women and children are inside the tunnel moving deeper and deeper to safety. Katsu runs to the mouth of the tunnel and peers down. He watches in sadness as the last of his Ninja companions are killed by multiple blades. The Commander looks up the elevation and orders, "Forward. Catch them!" Katsu takes one of the lit torches planted in a nook in the tunnel wall. He goes to a cord that is suspended from the ceiling and puts the flame to it - it sparks and becomes a burning fuse. Katsu with torch in hand turns and runs full speed into the depths of the tunnel, the glow of his torch disappears into the darkness. As the Commander and his troops reach the mouth of the tunnel - EXPLOSIONS! The Commander and soldiers watch as the tunnel becomes filled with massive boulders, stones and debris. The large rocks too heavy and too numerous to remove. The Imperial Commander and troops cannot pursue. The Commander yells and throws his helmet on the ground in a rage!

Dave Kwan

CHAPTER THREE
Capture and Destroy

The Imperial soldiers comb the villages and scour the mountain terrain looking for Ninja survivors. The soldiers find wounded Ninja and immediately kill them. With all Ninja survivors put to death, the villages are now under control of the Warlord's army. The Warlord and Castle Guards ride into the middle of the central village. The Ruler scans the ground littered with the dead bodies of soldiers and Ninja. A Commander runs over to the Warlord and presents him with a captured Ninja Banner. The Warlord grabs the pole and lifts the SHINOBI STANDARD high in the air for all his troops to see. His army repeatedly cheer! The Ruler beckons, and a nearby Commander rides to his side. The Warlord extends his arm in a sweeping motion, "Send troops to hunt down any Ninja survivors. Put posters across the land to say the Ninja are Outlaws. A reward for anyone that helps to capture them." The seasoned Commander nods and rides away. The Warlord and his Castle Guards ride off toward a large tent that's been erected on level ground. The Ruler stops at the tent entrance and attendants scurry out to assist the Ruler to dismount and tend to his horse. The Monarch enters the shaded confines of the ornate tent. Personal servants remove his gold armour and battle gear. A servant brings a gold silk robe and the warlord puts it on. Inside the tent, servants have laid out drinks, fruits, meats and pastries on a table. A servant pours a cup of refreshment and extends the goblet to the Warlord. He takes the cup and drinks back the liquid, wipes his lips with his sleeve - then flings the goblet away.

Across the land, Imperial soldiers put up posters in villages, markets, towns and fishing ports. The Japanese gather to read the Warlord's Edict. Many are shocked at the news while others relish the reward being offered. The soldiers search the towns and countryside. Troops stop carts and wagons to examine contents and passengers. Armed Officials enter homes and farms looking for any Ninja. In one town, the soldiers stop a group of travellers and discover they are Ninja. A fight breaks out as the Ninja defend themselves against the Imperial soldiers. The small band are fierce and deadly with their Ninja skills. An alarm is sounded and scores of troops rally to overpower and kill the Ninja men, women and children.

Twenty years pass.

Deep in the woods, the Sword Master now an old man, watches the grown man Takeshi at a homemade forge with glowing coals. Takeshi hammers the red hot metal into the shape of a curved Katana blade. The man grinds the metal blade and hones the edge to create a Ninja sword. The Sword Master inspects the blade's straightness, balance and sharp edge. The old man smiles and gives the sword back to his son. Takeshi is proud of his accomplishment and basks in the glow of his father's expert approval.

A modest thatch hut sits secluded in the forest. The peasant family go about their chores. This is the Sword Master's family living in disguise. Katsu is a fit wiry old man who chops wood logs into kindling to sell in town. Aiko, is no longer the young mother of yesteryear; now, she is a serene old lady content to weave baskets for market. She finishes a basket and hands it to Takeshi. He slips it onto the long pole from which other baskets hang. Takeshi lifts the pole to balance on his shoulder - baskets are in the front, baskets hang in the back. He looks at his mother, "I'll take the baskets to market now. Hopefully, we can sell them all." Aiko brushes straw debris from her skirt, stands up and looks at Takeshi, "Be careful in town! Remember - we are just simple peasants. No one must know who we are. Especially, watch out for robbers!" Takeshi adjusts the pole to a better position on his shoulder, "Don't worry mother. I know how to act (smiles) I will be back soon. If I meet robbers, my Ninja skills will destroy them - Father taught me well." Aiko manages a faint smile. She watches her son leave and walk the dirt path. Takeshi waves to his father who waves in return. Rei walks in from their large garden carrying eggplants, cucumbers, and green beans, and sets them into baskets for cleaning. She looks at her mom and remarks with a slight pout, "I want to go to market too. Why can't I go?" Aiko moves to stand beside her and lovingly strokes the daughter's long hair and pretty face, "Some soldier or Official may decide you should be his bride and take you away. - You don't want that do you?" Rei replies, "No mother. Never! Someday, I will marry a Ninja warrior and have my own family." Aiko's eyes linger on her daughter, "I wish that for you with all my heart, my daughter. (Pause) The Ninja are so few and so scattered, we are still hunted as Outlaws and must hide." The mother and daughter sit down to clean the vegetables. Katsu stops chopping wood, sets the axe aside and walks in to join them. He's hot and sweaty and dips a ladle into a barrel of water and brings it to his mouth and drinks slow and deliberate to quench his parched throat. The old man glances at Rei and Aiko to comment, "The wood kindling will sell well in market. Wood for fires and fires to cook food (he smiles) everyone needs to eat!" Katsu walks back to the wood pile and begins to sort and tie the kindling into bundles.

Takeshi walks along the countryside road to market. The long pole fitted with woven baskets bounces with his every step. Far up the road Takeshi spots a large mounted unit of Imperial soldiers riding toward him. Takeshi stops and moves off the road to the side and bows respect. The long column of soldiers get close, the hooves of the galloping steads dig into the dirt roadway. The soldiers glance at Takeshi as they ride past him. When the armed force have gone by, Takeshi stands upright. Others are also on their way to market - an ox cart filled with crates of chickens, some men lead a herd of sheep, women carry bolts of fabric, and teenagers walk with baskets of fruit.

Later on that day…

Imperial soldiers hide in foliage and observe the thatched hut with bundles of kindling stacked at the dwelling's side. Puffs of smoke drift from the roof's centre opening. No one is visible, there's no activity. Suddenly, Katsu, Aiko and Rei emerge from the hut. The Imperial Captain turns to a nervous fidgety man in tattered clothes and hands him a bag of coins. The man snatches the pouch of money - bows low - and quickly runs off into the woods. The Officer raises his arm and the soldiers attack! Aiko and Rei are alarmed and afraid. The Sword Master runs to a wooden trough and pulls out two Katana swords. He runs directly at the soldiers. The aged Ninja warrior swiftly cuts down the attackers - Katsu powerfully swings his Ninja swords and delivers deep cuts, and terrible slashes that sever limbs and leave mortal wounds. The blood flies! Soldiers topple like dominoes - dead or gravely injured. The old Ninja stands battle weary, dead bodies and bloody soldiers lay around him. The Captain barks an order and soldiers with bows form a line. The archers pull back their bows and shoot a barrage of arrows at the old man — six arrows strike him in the chest and torso. With gasping breath, Katsu looks over at Aiko and Rei. Mother and daughter freeze in horror as they watch the old Ninja Master drop dead to the ground. They scream! The soldiers swiftly seize and tie them up. The Imperial Captain strides over and stands next to Rei who looks to the ground, her hair covers her face. The Officer lifts his hand to part Rei's hair and behold her beauty. He pivots about and motions the soldiers to take away the female prisoners.

Takeshi walks the well trod earthen path through the forest towards home. He notices many broken branches and large patches of trampled grass. Takeshi gets alarmed and races toward the thatched hut. As he breaks through the woods, the bodies of dead soldiers litter the homestead clearing. He quickly looks around, and to his horror, he sees his dead father in the middle of a pile of slain soldiers. Takeshi runs and kneels over his father's body and stares at the six arrows sunk deep into the chest and torso. Tears run down his cheek and drop onto the Ninja Master's face. Takeshi gently lifts and carries his dead father into the thatched hut. Moments later, Takeshi emerges with a flaming torch in hand. He turns to look at their homestead and lifts his arm to throw the firebrand, and memories of happier days with father, mother and sister cross his mind - he hesitates; then he throws the flaming torch high onto the dry grass roof. Within seconds, flames swiftly spread across the roof to engulf the entire wood and hay structure. The flames shoot high in the air and smoke rises in the sky. Takeshi stands stoic and silent as he watches their family home burn. He turns and walks to the area of trampled grass and broken branches. Takeshi spots fresh tracks of flatten grass that lead away from the clearing. He sets out in that direction.

Aiko and Rei sit bound together in the back of an Imperial Prisoner Wagon A squad of soldiers guard them. The town's market is full of people buying goods from merchants and suppliers. Drivers steer animals pulling laden carts, venders hawk their wares to those walking by, street artists perform for the crowd, and beautiful maidens stroll together. Takeshi moves in and out amid the crowd until he's next to the Prisoner Wagon. The soldiers guarding the wagon become distracted by some passing maidens. He sees Aiko and Rei leaning against the metal bars - their eyes meet. Takeshi opens his tunic to reveal a knife handle - he nods. His mother's face shows worry and she shakes her head - No! One of the soldiers pushes Takeshi to move along and Takeshi's tunic opens and the knife handle is exposed. ALARM! The soldiers try to stop him and he uses the blade with Ninja skill - and kills them all. Takeshi quickly uses the big knife to snap off the back lock. He enters and cuts the ropes off his mother and sister. Takeshi and Rei jump out and turn to help their weaken mother get down. - Suddenly, two garrisons of soldiers race toward them. Armed reinforcements. The townsfolk scatter. Aiko is exhausted and looks into Takeshi's eyes, "I have no energy to run!" Takeshi pleads, "Mother, we must quickly flee! If they catch us - we die!" The mother reaches her hand to touch her son's cheek, "You are the last of our Clan. Go! Find someone to teach our Ninja ways.(Aiko cries) Hurry! Before it is too late - and our Ninja ways perish with us. Go!" The troops are close now. A group of soldiers stop and raise their bows to shoot arrows. Takeshi, Aiko and Rei, are crouched together beside the wagon. WHOOSH! Arrows fly around them, some strike the wagon. Aiko clasps Rei's hand and looks into her daughter's eyes - Suddenly, Aiko and Rei stand up to block and protect Takeshi. Arrows hit Aiko and Rei and kill them. Takeshi is SHOCKED! He looks at his dead mother and sister, then he sees the soldiers racing forward, he quickly runs to escape over a wall. The soldiers reach the Prisoner Wagon where Aiko and Rei lay dead, and keep running to go over the wall in hot pursuit. On the other side of the brick wall, the Garrison Captain and his men face a number of narrow streets and laneways. A soldier asks the Captain, "Which way did he escape?" The Captain scans the numerous passageways and orders, "Search them all - we must capture him!" The soldiers disperse in various groups and scour the buildings, streets and laneways.

CHAPTER FOUR

Ship to America

The wharf is packed with cranes and crews as cargo is loaded and unloaded onto ocean going ships. The big boats are berthed alongside the wide wharf, sailors scamper up and down rigging, some ships have sails unfurled while others have their vast canvass sheets lashed secure. Sailors and passengers walk up and down gangways. Piles of stacked crates cover the long dock. In this busy crowd, Takeshi stands opposite a Japanese Sea Captain. Takeshi glances over his shoulder to see if things are still safe, "I need a ship that will leave Japan." The Sea Captain, a portly man in his 50's looks at Takeshi and draws a puff of tobacco from his long narrow pipe, "Where do you want to go? Hong Kong? England? - Australia?" Takeshi glances around the crowd and replies, "I want to go far from Japan. Somewhere different!" Takeshi reaches into his tunic and brings out an exquisite piece of jade and hands it to the man, "I will trade this jade heirloom for passage." The Sea Captain's eyebrows raise, his eyes light up. He examines the fine quality of the jade, then he smiles at Takeshi and points, "That boat sails for America - a new country very different from Japan. The Captain is my friend, I will tell him you'll be a passenger. The Sea Captain takes Takeshi through the people and over to an old veteran Sea Captain. The man whispers into the old sailor's ear and shows him the jade. The old man looks at the jade and his friend, then he looks at Takeshi, smiles and nods - Yes! The old Sea Captain takes a few steps forward, turns to Takeshi and beckons to follow. Takeshi walks with the Captain along the wharf until they reach a large ship moored by the dock. The old sailor ascends the planks of the gangway and motions for Takeshi to join him. Takeshi grabs the safety ropes and walks up the gangway onto the ships's deck. The old man smiles and points to a set of stairs that lead below. Takeshi stands at the top of the stairs to survey what's beneath, he glances around and descends below deck.

Days and nights pass. The ocean changes from high winds and crashing waves, to calm waters and gentle breeze. Takeshi stands at the ship's bow as it cuts through the water, it's large sails catch the wind propelling the vessel at a good clip. Takeshi smiles as he sees dolphins racing alongside, leaping in and out of the ocean keeping pace with the ship's speed. He looks ahead at the far horizon and squints his eyes - the line between the ocean and the blue sky almost become unrecognizable, as if merging into one. He turns to observe the seamen busy at their post - swabbing the deck, rigging the jib and manning the lines. Takeshi looks at the ship's helm where the old Sea Captain stands next to a sailer steering the ship. He turns toward the distant horizon and closes his eyes and feels the warm ocean breeze on his face - and smiles.

It is morning and Takeshi ascends above deck just as the ship enters San Francisco harbour. Vessels from different countries flying their nation's flag line the long wharf. Excited immigrants disembark with suitcases, sacks, and possessions in hand. Takeshi's ship comes into position alongside the large wharf, and the sailors throw thick ropes to dock workers who tie and moor the ship in place. As people disembark the boat, Takeshi looks at the old Sea Captain, who gestures his arm toward the wharf, nods his head and smiles. Takeshi bows to the Sea Captain, then turns and walks down the gangway onto the wharf teeming with workers, sailors, passengers and immigrants. Takeshi moves with the crowd as people mill and jostle about, each making their way to destinations known and unknown. As Takeshi walks the wooden planks of the wharf, a mother carrying her baby suddenly drops a package on the boards, and she bends down to pick up her goods. To avoid stepping on the lady, Takeshi quickly sidesteps - and accidentally bumps into Cutter, a tall grizzled man in cowboy hat that holds a saddle in one hand and a Winchester rifle in the other. Cutter scowls with a mean stare, pushes the saddle hard to shove Takeshi aside, then continues his stride through the crowd. Takeshi regains his composure and makes his way off the wharf onto a busy city street. San Francisco is a bustling port city. Ships load and unload cargo, vendors hawk their wares, streets are clogged with horses, buggies and wagons, people mill about buildings, shops and saloons. Takeshi walks the city streets observing the sights and sounds. It's early evening and dusk has arrived, Takeshi walks down a street lined with saloons on both sides of the road. He happens to stop at the entrance of an alley between two buildings and hears a commotion down the pathway. Takeshi turns to see a middle-aged man on his knees begging for his life as Cutter holds a pistol against the man's forehead. The desperate man pleads, "Mister, I'm sorry! Powerful sorry for anything that offended you. Please don't shoot me!" The man on his knees turns his eyes toward Takeshi standing at the edge of the alley. Cutter notices the man's diverted gaze and turns to see Takeshi, then refocuses his anger at the man kneeling, "It's not what you did that offends me, it's what you are - a nobody! A pitiful excuse for a man." Cutter cocks back the gun's hammer. The man pleads with all his might, "Mister, please don't kill me - I have a wife and children. We're just homesteaders looking for land." Cutter grins, eases back the revolver's hammer and takes the gun barrel off the man's forehead, "Don't worry partner. You're not going to die on your knees today." Cutter steps back and holsters his gun and the man gets up and stands to his feet. Cutter turns and gives Takeshi a cold stare - then Cutter draws his pistol and shoots the man dead, his body falls to the ground with a thud. Cutter pivots and stares at Takeshi - Takeshi turns away and walks on down the street disappearing from the alley entrance. Cutter smirks and holsters his pistol, steps up to the dead man's corpse and kicks it, "Said you wouldn't die on your knees!" Cutter walks out of the alley and enters a nearby noisy crowded Saloon. The Saloon is a wild and boisterous place full of drunken patrons - rowdy sailors, dapper gamblers, ragtag miners, wild cowboys and flirtatious dance girls. Cutter pushes his way up to the bar and stands beside a rough gruff hombre. Cutter slaps the countertop to get the barkeep's attention, "Give me a Whiskey!" The barkeep brings over a short stout glass and pours a shot. Cutter grabs the barkeep's arm, "Leave the bottle." The barkeep sets the bottle down and goes to serve others at the bar. Cutter grabs the shot glass and belts back the amber liquid and slams the empty glass on the counter. The man next to him extends his glass and Cutter fills both glasses. Cutter holds up his shot of Whiskey and looks at the man beside him, "I'm heading inland - gonna start me a gang! Gonna rob, pillage and get rich." He belts back the liquor. His companion pipes up, "Easterners. Settlers. Farmers. All easy targets." Cutter reaches down and pulls out his pistol and spins the chamber, "This is the only Law out West! I aim to do as I please - Plenty of shootin' and killin' - and no one's gonna stop me!" The man beside him nods and grins. Cutter pours them both another shot and they belt back their drinks. Cutter slams the empty glass on the countertop. The barkeep comes over and remarks, "That'll be two bits for the bottle." The Cutter pulls out his pistol and lays it on the counter with the barrel pointed at the barkeep's belly. Cutter gives a mean look and sneers, "What did you say?" The barkeep stares at the gun barrel and replies timidly, "The Whiskey's free - on the house." Cutter nods and smiles. The barkeep quickly leaves for the far end of the long bar. Cutter looks at his tough friend and lifts his gun off the counter, and boasts, "This is what people understand - what people fear!" Cutter slaps the man's back and motions to leave. The two ruffians shove and jostle their way through the drunken crowd and out the Saloon's swinging front doors.

CHAPTER FIVE

San Francisco Chinatown

Takeshi works his way through the backstreets until he comes across wooden signs with Chinese Characters - He has discovered San Francisco's Chinatown. Asian immigrants have journeyed to America in search of a new life. Takeshi sees Chinese men and women, but most are transient men from China, South East Asia, Indonesia, Thailand and Singapore; husbands, fathers, brothers, sons - they have left their country with dreams of finding gold, work, or a piece of land to call their own. The Orientals mingle together in the fledgling shanty town at the outskirts of San Francisco proper. The Chinese immigrants have created their own community complete with stores, restaurants, laundry, hostels; and a gold exchange for the scores of Chinese miners that return from the mines with gold nuggets in their possession. Takeshi slowly meanders along the wooden boardwalk and peers in the open doorways that reveal Asian life that he's seen before - families at tables with bowls of rice, vegetables and soup, mothers with babies bundled to their back, groups of young men talking and drinking, young women washing clothes and folding laundry, and old men read newspapers and smoke tobacco from bamboo water pipes. Takeshi stops an approaching man, "Room? Rent?" The middle-aged man shakes his head, No, and keeps on walking. Further up the street, Takeshi stops beside three young men who are standing there smoking and talking, "Pay room?" The young men look at him, shake their heads and point down the street. Takeshi nods, and goes in that direction. As he moves a distance down the road, he nears a wooden two storey building and makes eye contact with an old man sitting quietly on the porch bench. He approaches the old timer, "Room. Pay!" The old man points to the building's wall behind him, "This is a Boarding House. Rooms to rent." Takeshi comes up onto the porch and sits beside the elderly man, "How?" The old man's face gets a wide grin and he chuckles, "My sister owns this building - I'll take you inside and you can ask yourself?" Takeshi nods and points to his chest, "Takeshi. Takeshi Shinobi." The aged fellow stops for a second, "Takeshi is a Japanese name." The old man pauses then smiles, "My name is Chow Zu Fu. I come from Guangdong, China." Takeshi replies, "Iga, Japan." Chow Zu Fu eyes Takeshi, "Everyone in America has left their homeland. Everyone is the same." The old man and Takeshi get to their feet and the man shuffles to the building entrance, stops and gives Takeshi a glance, "I moved quick like a fox when I was young, but now I move like a turtle." Takeshi replies, "You wise!" The old man's eye's brighten, "You're pretty wise yourself for a young man." Takeshi smiles, "Father. Mother." The old man taps his finger on Takeshi's heart, "You carry a treasure that's better than gold." The old man opens the door handle and they both step inside the building and walk to the side where an elderly lady sits behind a modest counter. The lady is wearing a ruby red silk dress and her silver hair is pinned up with a lacquered comb that features painted song birds. She looks up at Takeshi, while her brother leans in over the counter, "This man wants a room." The lady peers at Takeshi, "The rooms are five bits a week - if you like - two bits a night." Takeshi nods and holds up one finger. The old lady remarks, "One night?" Takeshi shakes his head. She utters, "One week?" Takeshi nods his head and smiles. The old lady nods agreement and extends her hand with open palm, "Pay before getting the room." Takeshi smiles and slips his hand into his trousers and brings out five coins in his hand. Old lady Lee takes the money, opens a carved ivory box and puts in the coins and closes the lid. She reaches her arm under the backside of the counter and produces a key on a leather cord, "Room 15. Upstairs in the back hallway." Takeshi takes the key, turns to the old man and smiles, "Talk. Good." Takeshi climbs the stairs to the second floor landing. He looks down at the old man and his aged sister at the counter, then he turns and walks the hallway to the back corridor and looks at the room numbers. His room is located on the right and he goes down the back hallway and stands before his new temporary home - Room 15. Takeshi inserts and turns the key - Click! He opens the door and gazes about the darken quarters lit only by shafts of moonlight coming through the window. Takeshi sees a kerosene lamp on a small nearby table, and picks up the matches and lights the lamp's wick - immediately light floods the room. Takeshi replaces the glass cover and sets the lamp on the table. He looks about the modest room - it has a single bed with a simple cabinet with washbasin on top and a little table with a kerosene lamp. The accommodation is small, simple, and spartan.

Early next morning, Takeshi is at the docks watching gangs of men load and unload cargo. He approaches a rotund man in his 60's sitting on a crate puffing a big cigar. He ambles over and stands close by. The portly boss barks to his crew, "Be careful with those crates! That's glass." The workers handle the cases with more care after receiving his rebuff. The man glances over at Takeshi, "What do you want?" Takeshi looks into the man's eyes and points to the workers. The man gives a quick look, then turns back, "You want work?" Takeshi smiles and nods firmly. The stout man gets off the empty crate and comes up to Takeshi to grab and squeeze his forearms and biceps, "You're strong enough - you'll do." He looks into Takeshi's eyes, then points to the closest crew that's busy carrying cases up the gangway to the ship, "You can work with them." The man waves to a large black man walking down the gangway and he comes over. The black man asks, "What do you want boss?" The boss flips his thumb at Takeshi, "He's on your crew so give him some work - report back how he does." The black man wipes sweat from his brow, eyes Takeshi and motions to come along. Takeshi follows and the crew chief shows a large pile of wood boxes and points to the ship, "Move these boxes onto the boat." Takeshi nods and quickly picks up a box and goes up the gangway to deposit the box on deck. He hastens down the gangway and continues to move the crates. The black man rejoins his crew and keeps his eye on Takeshi's progress. Later around noon, the black man notices the pile of wood cases have dwindled, and looks over to see Takeshi busy moving another box onto the ship. The black crew chief smiles as he continues to supervise his workers.

Through the years that he lives and works in Chinatown, Takeshi becomes involved in various jobs to earn the means to survive. He sells vegetables at the local market, and works at a Chinese Laundry shop washing, scrubbing and ironing customers' clothes; and he labours in a leather factory cutting, dying and sewing leather goods. As much as possible, Takeshi learns English from his co-workers and Chinese from the people of Chinatown. At the Chinatown Festivals, he watches the colourful celebrations complete with Dragon Dances and noisy fire crackers. One of Takeshi's favourite pastimes is to visit the local Kung Fu Schools and watch the teachers and students train to fight in Tournaments. Takeshi becomes familiar with the various Kung Fu fighting styles. Throughout it all, he still maintains his room at Grandma Lee's Boarding House, however his kind friend Chow Zu Fu passed away a few years ago, but his sister, the old lady, still runs the place from behind the lobby desk. Who would have known on the evening Takeshi wanted a room, he would eventually become the longest tenant at the Boarding House. Over the years, Takeshi works hard and saves his earnings and often trades money with miners in exchange for gold nuggets. No one knows except he and the old lady, but Takeshi stores small pouches of gold nuggets in a leather duffle bag that is locked away safe in a private room in the basement of the Boarding House.

Five years pass...

The wood steps creak as Takeshi walks up from the basement of the Boarding House, the large black leather duffle bag is slung over his shoulder. He walks over to Grandma Lee, napping with her eyes closed. Takeshi clears his throat to announce his presence. The old lady's eyelids flutter and she looks up to see Takeshi standing before her, "Are you off to work?" Takeshi gazes fondly at her, "Grandma Lee, I travel to the Great Plains." The old lady ponders a couple seconds for his words to sink in, "You are leaving us - leaving your home?" Takeshi nods and reaches into his bag and brings out a small pouch and places it before her wrinkled face, "You and your brother made me feel at home while I stayed here. Thank you Grandma Lee - this pouch is for you." The old lady clasps the pouch and brings it close. She opens the drawstring and sees the gold nuggets and looks up. Takeshi smiles, then he turns and walks across the lobby and out the Boarding House front door. Grandma Lee gets off her perch and goes to the window and peers out and watches as Takeshi disappears through the people and the busy street of Chinatown.

CHAPTER SIX

The High Sierras

From an elevation, Takeshi looks back at the port city of San Francisco spread out before him, the settlement buildings, stores and homes, the Bay and its water that leads the ocean, and the many ships anchored in the harbour. Takeshi turns around and moves to rejoin the long line of travellers making the hard climb over the Sierra Mountains. The terrain changes from the farmable soil in the lowlands, to the pebbles, stones and rocks of the highlands, then it becomes the huge boulders, cliffs and outcrops of the high elevations where the nights are bitter cold and the air gets difficult to breathe. Slowly, carefully, the line of pilgrims climb up the high Sierras; men, women and children, young and old, people of various nations, all in the quest for opportunity and a fresh start. On route, various groups of travellers cross paths, groups seeking San Francisco and the California coast, and those trekking across the mountains toward the Great Plains of the American West. On the journey, Takeshi encounters mountain men with furs, miners and prospectors with shovels and pick axe, families of homesteaders in wagons laden with possessions, Cowboys packing six guns, traders and vendors hawking wares, weary looking railroad workers, and lone drifters. As the columns meet each other on the Trail, there's no time to exchange conversation or have friendly banter. Whenever people made eye contact, nothing had to be said because everyone understood - all were simply moving on, searching, inwardly yearning, looking for that special place where they could build a better life.

One cold morning on the back side of the Sierras, there's a buzz among the people, voices of excitement, whispers of relief and outbursts of happiness. Takeshi strides toward the large group assembled on a wide rock ledge overlooking the horizon. As he works his way to the front of the people - his eyes widen and his heart races - there before him is land as far as the eye can see, - vast sections, an ocean of land, with enough space for families to build homes, good ground for farms and ranches, enough territory for entire towns. This is the Great Basin of the American West. A succession of hills and watersheds that lead to a territory with wide open plains and seas of rolling grass, a place known as the Great Plains - home to Native American Indians.

Having made the descent from the Sierras, the group that Takeshi travels with disperse, some are part of homestead groups, while others simply go their own way. Takeshi sets out across the Plains with duffle bag slung firmly over his shoulder, his stride deliberate and with purpose, his steps sure and steady. He notices the landscape, vegetation and creatures are different that his native Japan - the sage brush, the cactus, the Juniper tree, desert rattlesnakes and vultures. What intrigues Takeshi greatly are the wild mustangs he observes from time to time as he hikes across the land. He watches the herd with fascination and takes delight in the spirited nature of the horses - so wild and free. Takeshi camps out under the stars, the glow of his campfire keeps the animals at bay, the only sound are crickets and the lonesome cry of a coyote.

As Takeshi moves on, the ground ahead becomes rugged and rocky and he enters an area with pine trees, thick brush and hard rock terrain. Suddenly - DYNAMITE BLASTS. Takeshi turns to where the sound came from, and with curiosity Takeshi heads in that direction. He navigates between the pines and rugged gullies - only to emerge on the top of a rocky escarpment. Takeshi stops to behold the spectacle - hundreds of men labour under the hot sun to build new railway tracks through rock cuts. He looks at workers who are sweaty, dirty and tired. The work pace steady, the scattered groups resemble busy ants. From his high vantage point, Takeshi watches as teams of men clear ground, shovel gravel, carry heavy iron rails, lay thick timber beams, and hammer spikes to secure rails. Up ahead at the front of the work, are Chinese workers who place and light the dynamite - they also have the precarious job of carrying the volatile nitroglycerin. However, at this moment, no work is being done at the front section of the track. The Chinese and their Foreman have stopped and all stand idle. Off on a hill at the opposite end of Takeshi's position, is the Operation Tent and inside is Buford Pick, a mean gruff Railroad Boss whose background is ex-military. Pick's tall stature intimidates others as he leans over them barking orders that make subordinates cringe. Buford stands with his hand on the mounted brass telescope, as he scans across the railroad operation. He looks closely at everyone - Foremen and workers alike - no one can escape his steely gaze, he scrutinizes every person's effort. Buford Pick is someone greatly feared - his word is Law! Buford pans the telescope across the work and abruptly stops. He steps back and flips the telescope down in anger, "What are those Orientals doing down there? I told Jackson to keep up the pace. Now, they've fallen behind." Fuming mad, Buford turns to a man that stands to his side, Pick yells, "Boys! Ride down there and put those Chinamen back to work. I'm not paying them to stand around." The man gives a quick nod and exits the tent and immediately goes over to a bunch of rough mean-looking cowboys. This group is the Barlow Gang, a bunch of ruffians that stand ready to do Pick's bidding. They're uncouth, ill-tempered brannigans, always eager to dispense the Boss's justice. The leader injects, "Bout time we get to knock some heads together - can't stand this waiting around." One man remarks, "Never beat one of those pigtails before. YEHAW! Let's have some fun!" The Barlow Gang mount up and swiftly ride down the hill to the tracks below and race their horses to the front section where the Chinese workers are. As the Chinese workers are gathered together, the ruffians ride in and quickly dismount and begin to rip into the group - shoving, punching and kicking. The Chinese workers scatter to safe positions yards away. The Gang leader yells out, "Bossman doesn't like the hold up! What in tarnation is going on?" A fellow ruffian bellows, "Get back to work pigtails!" Out from the ranks steps Guan Yet Dee, an elderly Chinese man with braided white hair and a long white beard, "Velly Solly. No work. Velly Solly!" A gang member raises his boot and shoves the old man aside. The elderly man steps back and looks at Jackson. The Foreman steps out to stand beside Guan Yet Dee, and looks at the Gang leader and remarks, "The Chinese workers are scared of the nitro! They won't carry the nitro jars." The Barlow Gang look around menacingly at the workers clustered in separate groups. The cowboy leans forward, "Well, what happens when they carry the nitro?" Jackson glances about his workers and looks at the Cowboy leader, "They blow up! The Chinese get blow to smithereens!" His remark makes the Barlow Gang break out laughing! The Chinese workers become agitated and start to speak loudly in their vernacular language, their arms wave in animated gestures of concern and anger. The ruffian leader quips, "You mean to tell me these pigtails can't carry a wooden box?" Foreman Jackson replies, "It's not just carrying the box - it's carrying the nitro in the hot sun. Nitro explodes when it's gets hot!" The Gang leader grabs the reins and spins his horse around to gaze fiercely at the Chinese, then spits out chewing tobacco, "What's all the fuss! We gots lots of Chinamen - so what if they gets blown up, we gots lots more!" The rest of the Barlow Gang mount their horses - pull out their pistols and rifles and cock back the hammers. Their leader threatens Jackson, "You get them back to work! If they won't work - we'll put a bullet in any pigtail that refuses. Let's ride boys!" The gang turn their horses around and ride out kicking up a dust. With the ruffians gone, Jackson looks around at his work crew, then he motions Guan Yet Dee over to him, "You tell them to work. No work - you die! (He points with his finger) Bang! Bang!" Guan Yet Dee waves his arm at the Chinese workers to gather around and he explains to them that they must go back to work - or be shot dead!

Through all this, Takeshi stands atop the wilderness ridge, his dark black garb in contrast to the clear blue sky. He unslings the black duffle bag and sets it by his feet, and continues to observe the entire railroad operation, and notes the track crews, supply carts, construction materials, and the area for the workers' tents. Takeshi looks toward the track's front portion and fixes his eyes on where the Chinese are busy toiling away.

CHAPTER SEVEN

The Chinese Workers' Camp

At night when the day's tough work is over, the Chinese Workers' Camp is a welcome refuge from the harsh labour. The weary men relax in tents, while others sit in small groups to talk and smoke pipes or cigarettes. In the centre of Camp, Chinese cooks prepare the evening meal of rice, meat and vegetables. The head cook steps away from the kettles and lifts his voice, "Everyone - Come on! The food is ready." The Camp responds with men coming out of their tents and others get up from their groups. They collect the tin plates and utensils, but many still prefer to use chopsticks to eat their meal. The men stand eager to receive their grub. As the men gather, one worker notices a lone dark figure at the far edge of Camp. The worker cries an alarm, "Intruder! Intruder!" All the Chinese workers stop eating and getting their food, and just stare at the solitary figure. No one moves. No one does anything. Out from the ranks steps the elderly Guan Yet Dee accompanied by several muscular men. The aged leader approaches within a few yards and stops and gently studies the newcomer. The strong men with him stand ready for any trouble. The old man speaks, "Greetings stranger! What brings you to our camp?" Takeshi scans the old man and those along to protect, then he raises his arm up and jingles a small pouch of coins, "I'm hungry and will pay for food." The elderly leader moves closer, but one of the strong men named Lion puts out his arm to block him, "Grandfather, how can we trust him? He's a stranger. We know nothing of him." Guan Yet Dee looks at him, "Lion, who are we to refuse a hungry man food. Do not Generals feed their captured enemies. This man needs to eat!" The old man moves aside Lion's arm and walks to within a couple feet and bows, "My name is Guan Yet Dee. You are welcome to join us for food." Takeshi replies, "Thank you for your hospitality! My name is Takeshi." The elderly leader's eye brows raise and he stares more intently, "Takeshi - that is a Japanese name." Takeshi replies again, "Yes Grandfather, it is a Japanese name - for I am Japanese." The elderly leader steps closer and extends his arms with open palms, "Japanese. Chinese. Out here everyone is the same. We all are far from home! Please - eat." Takeshi nods and bows respect and carries his gear as he follows the old man through the throng of onlookers toward the kettles of food. The leader motions and a cook dishes out a heaping plate of rice, meat and vegetables. As Takeshi reaches to receive the plate, Guan Yet Dee notices the newcomer looks physically tired and weary from trekking the wilderness. Takeshi turns and extends his free arm and offers the small pouch of coins, "I will pay as promised." Guan Yet Dee gently moves the arm with coins to Takeshi's chest, "The Railroad gives us more than enough food. They like their workers healthy and strong. What we have we share - no need to pay. Eat." Takeshi spots a log to sit on and starts to dig into the rice, meat and vegetables - savouring the food with every bite.

Lion, some strong men and others, are at the far side of the Chinese Camp. They are suspicious of the stranger they've just encountered. One man remarks, "I heard the stranger tell Grandfather - he is Japanese!" The others are shocked at the news and begin to murmur. Another man speaks up, "He's not Chinese - he should not be in the Chinese Camp." Members of the group nod their agreement. One nervous fellow remarks, "What if he's with bandits, and others are waiting for his signal to rob us." A fellow quickly blurts, "No one is getting my money. I'm sending it back home to my family in China." By now, the group is worked up and scared, they look at each other, then turn their attention to Lion. Lion stands up, squares his shoulders and sticks out his chest, "No one will steal our money. We are strong enough to stop any bandits (he scolds) remember your Kung Fu!" The men look with expectation at him, one asks, "What will you do?" Lion puts his arm on the man's shoulder, "I will force this Japanese intruder to leave our camp." A man quips, "What about Grandfather? He gave the stranger permission to stay." Lion gazes about the group with a determined look and remarks, "Grandfather is old and soft. He should have stayed in the quiet courtyards of China. This rough wilderness needs strong men like us!" With that statement, Lion sets off toward the other side of the Chinese Camp. The rest of the group follow him.

* * *

Guan Yet Dee and Takeshi are in conversation when Lion strides up with his group of followers. The entire Chinese Camp stop what they're doing and watch intently. The elderly leader stands and politely bows, "Lion, you looked unsettled. Is something wrong?" Lion in anger points his finger at Takeshi, "He is Japanese! He should not be here - he must leave!" By this time, all the Chinese workers have gathered around to see what will unfold. Guan Yet Dee cups his hands together to plead with Lion, "Lion, this man is our guest, a fellow traveller, someone far from home like us all." Lion huffs and kicks dirt to reinforce his point, "Grandfather, you are old and lack the strength to make him leave. But I am big and strong - my Kung Fu will make him run away." With those words, Lion steps back and assumes a Kung Fu fighting stance circling his arms in a menacing manner, taunting Takeshi to fight him. Takeshi turns and bows to the old man, "Grandfather, thank you for the kindness you've shown me! I'm sorry to have caused a problem in the Camp. I will take my things and go." Guan Yet Dee replies with a sad expression, "I too am sorry, Takeshi! Not all Chinese men value the honour and respect of ancient times." As Takeshi turns and makes his way through the Chinese workers, one of Lion's group shouts, "He has fellow bandits waiting to rob us! How else could he survive this wilderness unless he's part of a gang." With such words, the whole Camp becomes upset, workers start to voice their fear and worry. Takeshi continues to walk through the men when one of Lion's group throws a punch at him. Takeshi's reflexes are lightning fast, he dodges the punch and grabs the man's arm and flips him into the dirt. The attacker gets up embarrassed and angry. Suddenly, Lion and his four Martial Arts companions surround Takeshi, each takes a classic Kung Fu fighting stance. The rest of the Chinese workers back up and fan out to give lots of room to fight. Takeshi watches Lion and the other opponents circle him. He recognizes the different Kung Fu fighting styles he saw and studied when he lived and worked in San Francisco Chinatown. Takeshi knows that he's being confronted by the Kung Fu fight styles of - the Tiger, the Leopard, the Crane, the Snake and the Dragon. With attackers moving around him, Takeshi stands relaxed, he closes his eyes and concentrates, then Takeshi quickly assumes a Ninja fighting stance. Lion forms a Tiger claw with his fingers and forcefully swings and rips open Takeshi's garment at the shoulder. Lion strikes again but Takeshi jumps and spins to kick away Lion's hand. Takeshi pummels the big man with a flurry of blows that drop him to the ground moaning and groaning. The man with the Leopard style attacks with a series of swift strikes and Takeshi deftly blocks the strikes and kicks the attacker unconscious. Suddenly, the Crane, lunges in with a torrent of fluid jabs, strikes and punches. But Takeshi is quicker and he dodges the jabs, deflects strikes and blocks punches. Takeshi flips backward and kicks the Crane under the chin to knock him out. Takeshi lands on his feet - poised and ready. Only the Snake and the Dragon remain. Both men look at each other and attack in unison. Takeshi blocks the pointed spear hand of the Snake, but the Dragon's fist hits full force and Dragon powerfully kicks Takeshi in the groin. Severely struck, Takeshi is momentarily off balance and out of breath. He teeters briefly but quickly regains his footing. The Snake on his left, the Dragon on his right, both close in - however, Takeshi counterattacks. He runs and jumps high to deliver a powerful kick to the back that pushes the Snake forward into Dragon's mighty fist. Dragon's punch knocks out the Snake. Takeshi lands and turns about - Dragon is momentarily distracted. Takeshi hits hard with a flurry of blows that strike his opponent's vulnerable areas. Dragon collapses to the ground in heap. Takeshi stands alone - and victorious! The Chinese workers are amazed and have never witnessed this kind of fighting style. They question and murmur among themselves. The elderly leader approaches, "Takeshi, I saw the tattoo on your shoulder. I know what you are!" Takeshi pleads, "Grandfather, please do not tell anyone, it must remain a secret." The aged man reassures, "Your secret is safe with me. - Have a good journey wherever you travel." Takeshi bows, "Thank you Grandfather! I will not forget your kindness." Takeshi turns and walks to the edge of the encampment and disappears into the woods. The elderly leader looks over at Lion and the other Kung Fu fighters who are recovering from their beating and nursing their injuries. Guan Yet Dee turns and retires to his tent.

CHAPTER EIGHT

Frontier Town of Emerson

Takeshi walks over vast rolling grasslands and climbs to the top of a big hill and stops to rest. He looks out to see a frontier town, the wood frames of new buildings and the numerous wagons and horses speak of a growing community. As he approaches the town limits he sees a sun bleached chipped sign with the words - The Town of Emerson. Takeshi enters the settlement and walks down the dusty busy main street and notices the townsfolk, settlers and Cowboys. He sees railroad workers, soldiers and drifters, those getting supplies at the Mercantile and loading up their wagons, while others drink at the Saloon, eat meals at the Cafe, or get shaves and haircuts at the Barbershop.

Emerson is a major Station on the Stage Coach route. The Station is a complex of wood structures in the middle of town. A large building for passengers and travellers, a Blacksmith and Livery Stable for the horses and wagons, and a bunkhouse for the drivers and workers. Takeshi watches a Stage Coach race into town, the driver snapping the whip and the horses kicking up a trail of dust. The team of horses and the Stage Coach come down the dirt road and pull into the Station. The horses are tired, sweaty and breathing heavy. Station workers quickly come out and open the Stage Coach doors to assist the passengers stepping down. Takeshi resumes his exploration of the town and strolls the wooden sidewalk taking him past buildings and stores. He stops in front of a wood building with large glass windows and notices the sign above the front entrance - LAND REGISTRY OFFICE. Takeshi looks through the front window at the Land Registry Agent seated behind a large desk tending papers. He opens the front door and steps inside and moves to stand before the Agent. Takeshi voices his purpose, "I want to buy farm. You have farm?" A skinny man with wire frame spectacles peers up at Takeshi and adjusts his glasses. The Agent clears his throat, "Do you have money to buy a farm? We have farms for sale - Easterners tried homesteading but gave up." Takeshi pulls out a tan leather pouch full of dollar coins and jingles it, "I have money. Enough money for land!" The Agent takes the pouch, opens the drawstring and shifts coins with his fingers, "Appears you got more than enough for a farm!" The Agent takes out the correct amount and hands the pouch back to Takeshi, "Well, come over here and look at the map." The man pushes his chair back and walks over to a large territory map on the wall. Takeshi follows him, his eyes scan across the map. The Agent points with his finger, "This is the town of Emerson (Points to other spots) and these are the farms for sale." Takeshi studies the map and notices a farm located alongside a river. He taps the map at that spot, "I take. This farm good. - Water!" The Agent tilts his head and grins, "You picked a good one alright! Only a two hour ride from town and right beside a river." The Agent and Takeshi return to the desk, and the Agent opens a drawer and pulls out a Land Registry Document. The man writes in the purchase details - then stops at NAME and looks up with an inquisitive expression. Takeshi speaks up, "Takeshi. Takeshi Shinobi." The Agent replies, "Can you write that down, please?" Takeshi leans forward, takes a pencil and writes his name in English. The Agent writes TAKESHI SHINOBI as the registered property owner - stamps the Land Registry Seal - and hands the Document to Takeshi. Takeshi inspects the paper, folds and puts the Deed inside his tunic. He smiles and nods his heads, "Thank you Agent San!" The man remarks, "If there's anything else you need, I'd be glad to help." Takeshi goes over to the big glass window and points to a buckboard in the street, "I need wagon. Wagon and horses." The Agent grins, "That you do. You can get a wagon and horses at the Livery Stable. Ask for the Station Master." Takeshi bows, then opens the door and leaves. The Agent gets up and goes over to the Office window and watches Takeshi go up the street. The man returns behind the desk and flips open a Ledger and mumbles, "I wonder how long he's gonna last?"

CHAPTER NINE
The Stage Coach Station

Takeshi approaches the Station and climbs the wooden steps of the large veranda. He stands on the porch in the shade and hangs his head - he's tired. The Station door opens and out steps Blake "Boots" Connors, the Station Master. He's a tall rugged man in a well-worn Stetson that wears Cowboy boots with silver toe caps. Only his friends can call him "Boots", all the others respectfully call him, Mr. Connors. The man greets Takeshi, "Where you off to Mister?" Takeshi lifts his head to make eye contact. The Station Master stops speaking - momentarily taken back at seeing an Asian man before him. Takeshi replies, "I want wagon - horses for farm." Blake Connors lifts his hat and sets it back again, "We usually don't get your kind." Takeshi reaches into his tunic and pulls out a gold nugget, "I pay for wagon, horses. You take gold." The Station Master's eyes grow big and he takes the nugget and rolls it in his fingers. The man looks at Takeshi and smiles, "For you, Partner, we can find a wagon and a team of horses!" Takeshi slightly bows, "Thank you Connors San!" The Station Master turns and opens the door and yells inside, "Get out here! You got work to do. This man needs a wagon and horses." Quick as can be, Boy, a twelve year old Indian lad appears in the doorway. His clothes are tattered, his hair wild and messy, and he looks a bit undernourished. The lad chimes, "Yes Sir!" The young lad looks over at Takeshi, then waves his arm to follow. The lad takes Takeshi across the street to the large Livery Stable and leads him inside to stand before three empty wagons. The lad points to the last wagon near the wall, "That's the best one Mister! The wheels and springs are good and strong." Takeshi slides off the duffle bag and walks over to inspect and check the wagon's wheels, buckboard, seat and hitch. He nods and smiles at the lad, "Good! Very good." Next, the lad guides Takeshi to where the horses are kept and goes beside a tan Mare and pats her side, the horse neighs, "This Mare is nice and gentle. Easy to handle." Then the lad walks between some horses to a chestnut Morgan. Takeshi asks, "This one okay?" The lad looks at Takeshi, "This horse is strong and steady - real good for pulling a wagon." Takeshi smiles at the lad and comments, "Horses like you. Very good!" The lad tenderly brushes the coat of the Morgan, "I've been living in this stable since bossman Connors found me. Been around horses ever since." Takeshi looks at the young lad with compassion.

Outside the Livery Stable, the lad harnesses and hitches the horses to the wagon as Takeshi stands beside the front wheel. Blake Connors strides over and tips his hat, "Fine wagon and team of horses." Takeshi looks up at him, then reaches into his tunic and pulls out a pouch and gives it to the Station Master. Blake Connors opens the pouch and pours gold nuggets into his calloused palm, "This will do fine. Yes Siree!" Takeshi turns and lifts his arm to point at the lad, "I want boy! Help on farm." Blake Connors gives Takeshi one long stare, glances over to the lad by the two horses, then eyes Takeshi and exclaims, "That lad tends my horses and wagons and helps clean up the Stable. He's important to me!" Takeshi grabs the duffle bag and reaches inside and brings out a black leather pouch and tosses it to Connors, "For boy - much gold!" Blake Connors feels the weight of the pouch in his hand, then he opens the draw string to look inside - and takes out a big gold nugget. He sifts his fingers through the nuggets, grins and looks at Takeshi, "You want to pay this much gold for the boy! He's just some Indian kid I found wandering the brush." Takeshi turns to watch the lad gently stroke the Mare's forehead. He looks at Connors with determination, "You take gold! I take boy. Good!" The Station Master tips back his Stetson and bounces the pouch of gold up and down in his hand, he looks at the lad, then he looks at Takeshi with a big smile, "Mister, you got yourself a deal. Mind you - I'm getting the better part!" Takeshi throws the duffle bag into the cargo box, then he climbs up and takes a seat on the wagon. Blake Connors waves the lad to come over. Connors puts a hand on the lad's shoulder, "Boy, go get your clothes and things. You're going with this man here - You work for him now!" The Station Master turns and walks away. The lad looks up at Takeshi and stands there silent for a bit, then he turns and goes into the Livery Stable. Moments later, the lad returns carrying a few clothes, a rucksack, and a horse bridle. He climbs up into the wagon and sits beside his new boss. Takeshi grabs the reins to move out the horses, the wagon rolls away from the Livery Stable and Station. With the lad quietly beside him, Takeshi steers the wagon down Emerson's main street heading out of town. Blake Connors stands on the shaded porch and watches the wagon disappear out of sight. He holds the pouch firmly in his hand, "With this much gold, I could hire a bunch of Indian boys to work horses." He adjusts his Stetson, opens the front door and steps inside.

CHAPTER TEN

The Abandoned Farm

Takeshi and the young lad ride the wagon over the packed earthen road. The team of horses draw the wagon at a good clip. The lad watches a rabbit dart across the grass, he looks up at birds flying overhead, and notices a patch of wild flowers alongside the road. Takeshi glances at the lad then passes the reins over to him and smiles, "You drive now." The lad breaks into a big grin and takes the reins with gladness. As the lad coaxes the horses along Takeshi observes how the boy steers and handles the wagon. Takeshi sits back and pulls out the Property Document and studies it. The paper shows the road they're on, the river and the farm boundary. He returns the paper inside his tunic. The wagon passes through tree groves, across grassy meadows and along the slow moving river. As the lad steers the wagon and horses around a bend - the lad pulls the reins to stop. Takeshi and the boy sit transfixed beholding the farm property. It's located right near the river and the farm house looks decent and in good repair. A small veranda marks the front door. There's a modest barn with a corral that lays a hundred yards from the house. To the right near the river, are some oak and ash trees that stand as a windbreak and provide patches of cool shade from the hot sun.

The lad pulls the horses and wagon up near the house, jumps out and lashes the reins to the corral post. Takeshi gets down and walks over to inspect the farmhouse, the lad follows him. Takeshi and the lad walk to the front entrance and Takeshi opens the door and they both enter the clapboard structure. Takeshi and the lad gaze around at the interior - the Easterners abandoned in a haste and left their furniture and household goods behind. Whether it was the trouble of packing and trekking everything across the wilderness all the way back to the East Coast, or whether it was sheer discouragement and frustration that made them leave their possessions; whatever the reason, there in the farmhouse stood their homestead furniture and provisions. Takeshi steps over to a wood chair and draws his finger across the seat to make a line in the dust. He glances at the lad, "We clean. Very dirty - we make good. (Pauses) We put horses and wagon in barn." The lad nods and both exit the front door. The boy walks to untie the reins from the corral post and they walk the horses and wagon across the farmyard to the barn. The lad grabs the barn door and swings it open to reveal a mess of boxes, wood crates, junk and debris. Takeshi and the boy are taken back some, Takeshi remarks, "We clean barn too!" The lad leads the team into the barn and unbridles and unhitches the horses. He finds two feed bags that still have oats and sets it before the Mare and Morgan. Takeshi and the boy move the wagon into a better position. Takeshi looks about and spots two tin buckets near the inside wall. He goes over and picks up the buckets, motions to the lad, then they exit and close the barn door. The two walk toward the house when Takeshi stops a few feet before the veranda and turns to the lad and hands him the tin buckets, "Go to river. Fill with water." The lad runs with the buckets to the river, kneels down beside the riverbank and dips in one bucket at a time to fill with water. When both are full, he scoots back to Takeshi at the front door. Takeshi grabs a pail - opens the door and they both go inside. The lad watches as Takeshi rolls up his tunic sleeves and gets two clothes from the duffle bag - he tosses one cloth to the boy. They both begin to use the dry cloths to remove the layer of dust on the furniture and house interior.

Later on in the evening, one very tired young lad rests on his cot beside the far wall. The boy opens his eyes to see Takeshi at the fireplace with a good fire, he's bent over a kettle adding ingredients. Takeshi reaches into a bag and brings out more items to drop into the kettle, next he grabs a wood ladle and begins to stir the simmering water. He lifts up the ladle to taste the broth - Ahhhh! Takeshi looks over at the lad who now sits up alert and awake. Takeshi announces, "Soup ready. We eat." The lad gets off the cot and comes over to the wood table and sits down. Takeshi fills two bowls with soup and brings them over to the table and sets one in front of the boy, he hands the lad a spoon. Takeshi places his bowl on the table at the other end, sits down and starts to spoon the soup into his mouth. He lifts his eyes to observe the boy heartily devouring the soup - when finished the lad picks up the bowl and licks the inside. The boy looks at Takeshi and shows the empty bowl. Takeshi grins and motions to the kettle. He watches as the lad eagerly get up, goes to the kettle to refill his soup bowl, and returns to his chair and makes short work of his second helping. The young lad scoops out the last of the soup and tilts the bowl to lick it clean. The lad sets the bowl down and uses his sleeve to wipe his mouth. Takeshi smiles, gets up and walks to his cot against the opposite wall, sits down and stretches out to relax. The lad still tired, Yawns!, then ambles over to his cot and lays down. The burning wood in the small fireplace dies down and becomes radiant embers that cast a warm glow across the farmhouse interior, the golden light falls on the faces of Takeshi and the lad, both fast asleep from a very busy day.

Early next morning, the lad and Takeshi walk to the barn and commence to clean and tidy the structure. They lift and carry the boxes and crates and stack them orderly against an interior wall, then they shuffle sacks of grain to create more room in the middle. Afterwards, they gather all the discarded tools and assemble them in a spot near the Barn door. Takeshi grabs two shovels and places his hand on the lad's shoulder motioning that they leave. Walking out of the Barn, Takeshi leads the lad to an wide patch of open ground. The boy watches as Takeshi takes his shovel to dig and til the ground into clumps of overturned earth. He glances over to the lad and motions to do likewise. Under the early morning sun, Takeshi and the lad dig up the ground to create a big section of freshly tilled dirt. Takeshi hands the lad his shovel and leaves to go inside the house and quickly returns with a sack and one of the tin buckets. He takes out a sharp metal awl and pokes holes in the bottom of the bucket. Next, as the lad keenly watches, Takeshi puts his hand into the sack tied to his waist and brings it out full of seeds which he scatters across the tilled earth. Takeshi gives the bucket to the lad, "Get water." The boy scampers to the river, dunks in the bucket and brings the leaky pail back and hands it to Takeshi. The man begins to walk over the area with the leaky bucket and water drips onto the scattered seeds. He hands the bucket to the boy and motions to continue what was demonstrated. As the lad waters the dirt, Takeshi continues to scatter seeds across the patch of fresh turned earth. During their work, the lad makes several trips to the river to fill his pail and water the large patch of ground. At noon, the sun is high in the sky and very hot. Takeshi and the lad walk over to the leafy trees to rest in the cool refreshing shade.

It's evening and dark outside, there's a roaring fire and Takeshi has another soup in the kettle. He stands beside the kettle and adds greens, dried mushrooms and sprinkles of seasoning. He looks over at the lad sitting patiently at the table eager to eat. When the soup is ready, Takeshi brings over two full bowls and sets one in front of the lad. The boy grabs his spoon and digs in with a hungry youthful appetite. Takeshi sits down and takes a spoonful and slowly sips the broth as he watches the boy eat. As before, the lad quickly finishes his bowl and looks expectantly at Takeshi, who smiles and nods. The lad gets up and goes to the kettle to fill up another helping, then returns to the table and begins to eat. Takeshi observes the boy with a fatherly gaze. When the lad finishes his soup, he pushes the bowl aside and looks at Takeshi. Now that the lad has eaten, Takeshi arises and goes over to the big leather duffle bag, reaches inside and brings out a red pouch tied with a gold cord. He walks back to the table, sits down and opens the drawstring and removes an ink bottle, brush and a roll of parchment paper. Takeshi unrolls a section of paper, opens the small ink bottle and dips in the brush. He writes a Japanese Kanji on the parchment and blows on the ink. Satisfied the ink is dry, Takeshi holds up the paper and shows it to the boy who's been keenly watching. Takeshi points to the Japanese Kanji then points to the lad, "You - Minarai. New name for you. - Minarai." The boy's eyes lock onto the paper and he attempts to repeat the word, "Min-ar-ai. Minar-a. Minarai!" Takeshi nods and smiles approval, "Hai! Minarai. - I call you Minarai." Takeshi puts his hand into his tunic and brings out a small knife and cuts off the piece of paper and hands it to the boy. The young lad reaches for the paper and hold it up as his eyes trace the ink details of the brushwork. The lad smiles deeply, "Minarai. Minarai. Minarai." The boy gets off his chair and goes over to sit on his cot and stares at the paper. The flickering flames of the fire make shadows dance across the room. Even as Takeshi has gone to sleep, Minarai stares at the paper in the fading light.

It's morning and Minarai rolls out of bed and pulls his suspenders over his shoulders, he walks over and opens the front door. Takeshi is sitting on the veranda step whittling a piece of wood with his pocket knife. The lad looks intently at Takeshi who keeps shaving curls of wood off the stick. Minarai bends down to sit beside Takeshi and watches the man shape the wood stick into a handle. The man is aware of the young lad's curiosity so Takeshi looks at him, "Minarai. You hear story? My story? I tell." With Takeshi's broken English he rehearses his story for the lad. He talks about his family living in the Iga Mountains of Japan, and how a Warlord attacked his people killing many and sending the rest into hiding. Takeshi tells of crossing the ocean on a ship to America, and how he lived and worked in Chinatown where he traded money for gold nuggets. He spoke of the Railroad tracks and walking the wilderness to reach Emerson where he bought the farm, wagon and horses - and how he wanted to free Minarai and help care for him. Afterwards, Minarai sits fascinated hearing Takeshi's story. This was the most words and longest time that anyone ever spoke to Minarai before. Takeshi finishes speaking and glances at Minarai, "Enough talk - we fix barn." The two rise to their feet and walk past the corral toward the barn.

CHAPTER ELEVEN

Fight at the Mercantile

Two Months later…

Minarai drives the wagon and team of horses as Takeshi sits quietly on the bench beside him - they're going into town for supplies. The lad aptly handles the wagon as the horses trot along the dirt road past the grove of trees, through the meadow and over rolling hills - right into the town of Emerson. The wagon rolls past the Hotel, Barbershop, Saloon, Cafe, Land Office and Bank, until Minarai pulls the reins to stop the horses in front of the Mercantile. The lad pulls the brake handle and lets go of the reins. Takeshi gets out and stands on the boardwalk, he looks at his young friend, "Minarai, you stay wagon. I go see store." The lad nods, "Yes Sir!" Takeshi turns and enters the big general store, and scans around at the interior packed with various dry goods, hardware items and homestead supplies. He walks the thick wood planks and moves through the aisles of stacked merchandise. Takeshi sees - sacks of grain, barrels of straw brooms, crates of fragrant soap, bags of baking flour, boxes of nails, coils of rope, and bolts of fabric. The Mercantile stocks lots of items, almost anything you'd need to live in town, or on a ranch or farm. Takeshi collects 3 bags of seed, a bucket, an axe, 2 kerosene lamps, a coil of rope, and 2 candy sticks. He takes the items over to the long wood counter and lays them before the storekeeper. The man looks the items over and slides them to the side, "Will that be all? Takeshi smiles and gives a polite nod, "2 months - buy again." The storekeeper scribbles down numbers on a long list beside him and gives Takeshi his attention, "Well - everything comes up to three bits." Takeshi hands the man the money and he gathers the items up in his hands.

Minarai sits quiet and peaceful on the wagon bench waiting for Takeshi to return. A few buildings away, a rowdy bunch of Cowboys come out of the Saloon and start to proceed down the boardwalk. They are loud, noisy and really drunk. As the Cowboys approach the Mercantile, they see Minarai sitting in the buckboard. The Cowboys stop beside the wagon and begin to threaten and menace the young lad. Minarai has experienced drunks before and swiftly diverts his gaze to the ground. One drunk Cowboy bellows, "Look here boys - we have us an Indian!" A couple of the Cowboys move into the street to confront Minarai's attempt to look away. A couple fellas put their boots onto the wagon to intimidate. A Cowboy pipes up, "Where'd you get this wagon redskin? - Steal it?" Minarai is a skinny twelve year old kid while these Cowboys are big strong young men wearing holsters with guns. Minarai raises his eyes to glimpse around, then quickly lowers them. A Cowboy yells, "Maybe this Indian brat needs a whoop-in' to learn respect." One Cowboy climbs into the buckboard and roughly grabs the back of Minarai's collar. At that moment, Takeshi comes out of the Mercantile carrying the supplies. He sees what's happening and quickly lets go - the items fall onto the planks of the boardwalk. CLUNK! The Cowboys turn their attention to Takeshi who stands at the ready. A Cowboy snickers, "Well - wouldn't ya know it - a Chinaman!" The Cowboys break out laughing! One of their group remarks, "A mangy Indian kid and an ole Chinaman." The guy beside him barks, "Maybe we should whoop them both. Let's start with the old man - then the kid." All the Cowboys sneer and nod. They begin to move toward Takeshi. Great concern comes over Minarai's face, he's frozen in fear. Townspeople have stopped to see the fuss and commotion. Down the street a man runs into the Saloon and let's loose, "Hey everybody! The Cowboys are gonna lay a beating on someone." Everyone gets up and the Saloon crowd spills out into the street. The people scurry to the Mercantile. By now, quite a number of townsfolk are gathered in front of shops and buildings opposite the Mercantile. The Mercantile Storekeeper comes outside to try and stop the Cowboys, "Now see here - you bunch stop this! Clear out of here." One of the older bigger Cowboys shoves the Storekeeper back inside, "Not your fight old timer - stay outta this if you know what's good!" The overpowered Storekeeper sheepishly steps back into the safety of the store. The Cowboy leader strides over and throws a punch. Takeshi blocks the swing and thrusts his fingers into the nape of the neck, the ruffian crumples to the planks - Gasping! Two Cowboys attack, one kicks with his boot while the other throws a mean punch. As the young man kicks his leg, Takeshi grabs the boot heel and flips him backwards into the street below, then he turns to catch and powerfully torque the Cowboy's fist and flips him onto the wood planks. Thud! The three remaining Cowboys start to lunge - Takeshi jumps high and kicks one unconscious, then he lands with a roundhouse to blast the other down the boardwalk. Just one Cowboy left - he looks at his fallen amigos, he won't fight and raises his hands in surrender. Takeshi looks over at Minarai - the lad is stunned! Takeshi glances around at the large crowd of onlookers, many totally astonished at such a display. Takeshi goes near Minarai, "You okay? No hurt?" The lad replies, "I'm okay - didn't get hurt." Takeshi is relieved, "You safe. Good!" Takeshi gathers and loads the supplies. He climbs into the wagon, grabs the reins and lets loose a whistle and snaps the leather reins. The horses pull away from the Mercantile, the crowd of townsfolk watch as Takeshi and Minarai go down the street heading out of town. Many of the townsfolk still amazed at what they witnessed. As the Cowboys collect themselves and regroup, two of them full of anger, pull out their pistols and aim at Takeshi and Minarai. The two cock back the gun hammers ready to fire. BOOM! BOOM! Emerson's Sheriff, Marshall Miller and Deputies stand nearby with rifles raised. The Sheriff steps up and looks at the Cowboys, "Put away your guns! There's no shootin' around here." The Cowboys look hesitantly at each other, then the two Cowboys holster their pistols. The Cowboy leader approaches the Lawman, "Sorry Marshall! We were just having some fun - right boys?" All the Cowboys nod and feign innocence. The Lawman replies, "Alright then! Just remember you're in my town and I don't cotton to gunplay. Understand?" The Cowboys nod compliance, "Yes Siree, Marshall - we understand." Marshall Miller eyes the group, "Good! (Turns to crowd) Now everybody…" A loud gruff voice breaks through the air, "What's all the ruckus?!" Cutter and his gang stand on the boardwalk, each man tough and gritty with a rough mean appearance. The drunk Cowboy leader squints his eyes at Cutter then gives a surprised yell, "Uncle Cutter! - Is that you?" Cutter steps off the boardwalk and strides over to his nephew and slaps his back, "Last time - you were just a scrawny kid. Look at you now, all grown up." The nephew remarks, "I'm riding the cattle drive from Arizona (points about) We're together, just in town to let off some steam." Cutter grins at his nephew and looks at Marshall Miller. The Sheriff injects, "Those boys were about to shoot some fellas. Not in my town!" Cutter eyes the Cowboys then addresses the Sheriff, "Well, nobody got shot! - like the boy said - just letting off some steam. Don't fret Marshall, I'll take the lads with me (Cutter puts an arm around his nephew) We gots catching up to do!" Cutter and his gang and the Cowboys head toward the Saloon. Marshall Miller turns to the crowd of onlookers, "Okay everybody! Go back about your business - nothing to see here." The townsfolk, shopkeepers, farmers and drifters disperse and go back to their activities. Out on the road back to the farmhouse, Takeshi steers the wagon as Minarai sits quietly staring ahead, occasionally, Minarai looks at Takeshi with a pensive glance.

CHAPTER TWELVE

Minarai's Ninja Training

Minarai and Takeshi are sitting relaxed on the step of the veranda when the lad turns and asks, "You fought so many at the same time. How did you do it?" Takeshi stares out at the tree grove then looks intently at the boy, "You want fight like me?" Minarai stands up excited, "Yes! I want to protect myself...and help others too!" Takeshi fastens his eyes on Minarai who stands with nervous energy waiting a reply. Takeshi picks up a twig, bends his head down as he draws in the dirt, "What I teach very old - from Japan - Ninja very hard!" Minarai stiffens himself with determination, "Teach me, please! I'll work real hard!" Takeshi studies the young lad and sees the resolve in his eyes, "You good worker, I know, I watch (Pause) Ninja very hard - maybe you stop?" Minarai makes direct eye contact, "I can do it, and train hard too!" Takeshi ponders the boy's words and attitude, then stands up and puts his hand on the lad's shoulder and smiles, "Okay! You train Ninja!"

The next morning, Takeshi sits bareback on the Morgan as the horse trots along the road with Minarai running to keep up. Takeshi coaxes the horse into a slow gallop to pick up the pace and looks around at Minarai who's starting to strain and breathe heavy. Three miles further up the road, Takeshi stops the Morgan and waits - he dismounts and stands on the road looking for a sign of Minarai. Takeshi squints and sees Minarai as a tiny figure coming toward him. After many minutes, Minarai appears with a slow jog, the lad meanders to and fro on the road. Finally, when Minarai reaches Takeshi's spot, the lad wobbles over and collapses on the grass by the roadside gasping for breath. Takeshi walks over to where Minarai lays and watches the boy's lungs heave to get air. Minarai glances up and blurts out, "How did I do?"

Takeshi grins, "Okay start. Now run back!" Minarai eyes bug out as he fights for air, "Run back - now?!" The man bends down for eye contact, "Yes! Run to fight - fight to run. You run now!" Takeshi flicks Minarai's shoe and waves come on. Breathing heavy, Minarai stands to his feet and watches Takeshi climb onto the Morgan and turn the horse toward the farmhouse going slow. Minarai launches out and jogs beside Takeshi and glances up, "Glad I can rest tomorrow." Takeshi eyes Minarai with a stern look, "No rest - tomorrow you run - every day run - get strong!" Minarai can hardly believe his ears and has a bewildered expression, "Run again tomorrow! What about breaks - rest?" Takeshi smiles coy, "Train Ninja - run each day - train each day - get strong!" As the Morgan's gait increases, Minarai starts to fall further back with Takeshi going farther down the road, the lad mutters, "Run, get strong...get strong, run. (Pause) He doesn't want a Ninja - he wants a horse!" Minarai maintains a steady pace as he jogs alone on the road back to the farm. When he reaches the farmhouse, Minarai is hot, sweaty and tired. He slowly jogs past Takeshi at the veranda, past the farmhouse, and keeps jogging up to the riverbank and jumps into the cool water. Splash! As Minarai stands up waist deep in the river, he looks over to see Takeshi having a good laugh. The lad flops backwards in the water and just floats to let the refreshing river water cool him down. Later at the evening meal of rice, vegetables and rabbit, Takeshi hands Minarai a pair of short wood sticks. The lad holds the sticks in his fingers and watches Takeshi use his pair of wood sticks to pick up and place vegetables on top of his rice. Minarai asks, "What are these?" Takeshi scoops in a mouthful of rice and extends his hand and demonstrates opening and closing the sticks, "Chopsticks. Chopsticks to eat." Minarai positions his fingers like he sees Takeshi and attempts to pick up a piece of celery - it falls onto the table. The lad tries again - and again - and again - until finally, he can hold a piece of vegetable without dropping it. Takeshi smiles as Minarai pops the celery chunk into his mouth, "Good. Very good!" Minarai smiles at Takeshi's comment and the lad commences to carefully eat his bowl of rice by adding other ingredients. Both enjoy their steamed rice, savoury vegetables and cooked rabbit.

Minarai's regime for Ninja training not only has long distance running, but also includes learning to balance - on a tree branch, atop the corral fence, then with one leg on a wagon wheel. Minarai climbs overhand on ropes suspended from the barn to strengthen his arms. He stands motionless for long periods of time - in the hot sun and through the cold night. Month by month, the physical exercises help the lad to grow strong, tough and agile. As the seasons pass, and through the hard training and healthy eating, Minarai becomes taller and more powerful, no longer the skinny under-nourished kid that he was when Takeshi found him.

Seeing that Minarai is now fit and muscle-toned, Takeshi begins to instruct on how to hold and handle the wooden practice sword to attack and to defend. Being capable with the wood sword, Takeshi moves Minarai to train with the Katana - the steel sword. Minarai's aptitude and attitude impress Takeshi as the boy handles the steel sword with improved speed and skill. Next, Takeshi introduces his young apprentice to the other Ninja weapons - and in quick time, Minarai aptly proves himself with all the Ninja weapons - the staff, the sword, bow and arrow, chain dart, blowpipe, and the Shuriken - the sharp metal throwing stars. Takeshi teaches Minarai how to create poisons and explosions, and in the evening after their mealtime, the lad learns to read Japanese and the ancient Ninja scrolls.

One morning as Minarai walks out of the farmhouse ready for another day of Ninja training, Takeshi motions to accompany him. The both walk to a prepared area behind the barn where Takeshi has constructed a homemade forge complete with anvil, tongs, hammers, water trough, straight irons and waterstones. Minarai looks at the set up and asks Takeshi, "Master, what is all this?" Takeshi picks up a set of tongs and turns to the youth, "To handle the Katana sword is very good! - To know how to make a Katana sword is better! Minarai, you will learn how to make a Ninja sword." The lad's eyebrows lift and excitement fills his eyes. He stands and keenly observes as Takeshi begins the sword making process. Over the succeeding days, Minarai watches and studies how Takeshi works the bellows to heat the fire to melt the iron sand and coal, then pour the molten metal into a blade shaped cavity in an earthen cast. He notices how Takeshi hammers the red hot steel bar into a sword blade. The youth focuses on the way Takeshi grinds and hones the steel blade into a sharp shiny sword with a razor edge. When it's all finished, and the sword handle and scabbard are carved, painted and lacquered - Minarai is thrilled when Takeshi presents the completed Katana sword for him to examine. Minarai's hand respectfully holds the sword and brings in for a close inspection. The lad runs his fingers over the high gloss finish of the lacquered wood. He pulls the sword partly out and fixes his gaze on the polished steel blade and sharp edge - then Minarai extends his arm to fully draw the sword out of the scabbard and lifts the gleaming blade up in the air. Takeshi watches as Minarai swings and maneuvers the Katana with skill and quiet grace. As he returns the sword into the scabbard, the young man looks at Takeshi with a smile, "The Katana is beautiful! So well balanced in the hand." Takeshi looks at Minarai with a twinkle in his eye, "The Katana is yours! (Pause) You've trained hard - earned it!" Minarai breaks into a big happy grin and clutches the Katana with childlike delight as on Christmas morning, "The Katana is mine! - My own sword?" Takeshi nods. Minarai's eyes are lost on the Katana, then the young man turns to Takeshi and bows very low, "Arigato Sensi! Thank you Master!" Takeshi replies, "Time for supper. We rest in our home." The two make their way to the farmhouse, Minarai carries his new sword with deep pride.

CHAPTER THIRTEEN

Yuji - The Ninja Master

Ten years later…

Takeshi is dressed in an ornate Japanese kimono with embroidered trim and details. A long white banner with a large Japanese Kanji - SHINOBI, flows in the breeze. Bouquets of bright flowers decorate around a rectangular straw mat where Takeshi kneels. In front of him an exquisite crafted Katana sword sits in a wood cradle. Minarai kneels opposite Takeshi and wears a black Ninja outfit. Takeshi lights incense sticks and begins to chant Japanese words. When finished, Takeshi picks up the sword with both hands and offers it to the graduate. Minarai receives the sword and bows in respect. As Minarai is bowed low, Takeshi chants Japanese as he passes the burning incense sticks over the young man. The moment the chanting stops, Minarai raises upright and looks straight ahead. Takeshi takes a white paper with Minarai's name and burns it in a bronze bowl. Next, Takeshi takes a calligraphy brush and writes a Japanese Kanji - YUJI - on a piece of white paper in red ink. He holds up the paper and hands it to the graduated apprentice and remarks, "Your new name is Yuji - Good Son! From this day on you will carry the name Yuji." The young man bows and holds the sword extended with both hands, "Hai! Yuji. My name is Yuji!" Takeshi smiles fondly, then passes over all his Ninja weapons, possessions and the ancient scrolls to Yuji. The young man shows deep humility at such a great honour. Both arise to their feet and look at each other. Yuji bows to Takeshi who bows in return, they both stand peaceful and silent. After a moment that seemed to last forever, Takeshi gives Yuji a smile, then walks to the farmhouse, enters and closes the door. He leaves Yuji to stand as his own man - as a Ninja Master!

* * *

The following morning Takeshi sits at the wood table and looks at the tea cup, tea pot, small bamboo ladle, clean linen cloth, and the flower arrangement on the table. This morning is unlike all other mornings because Yuji is performing the ancient Japanese Tea Ceremony to honour his Teacher and Master. The older man watches carefully as Yuji masterfully executes each step of the Tea Ceremony with the utmost care. Takeshi and Yuji take up their tea cup and drink in respectful silence. After the Tea Ceremony is finished - and a quiet pause - both men stand up. Yuji crosses the floor and picks up the black leather duffle bag and slings it over his shoulder. He walks to the door, opens it and turns to Takeshi and bows low, "Arigato Sensi! Thank you Master for helping to raise and care for me! Thank you for teaching me to be a Ninja!" The old man and father-figure with quivering voice replies, "I have loved you as a son. I have taught you everything I know. Now you are ready to make your own way." Yuji answers with watery eyes, "I will never forget you Sensi!" Yuji bows to Takeshi one last time, then the young man exits and quietly closes the door. Takeshi sits down and claps the tea cup with a smile of deep contentment and happiness!

CHAPTER FOURTEEN
Yuji Walks Shoshone Lands

Yuji walks across plains and grasslands and through wilderness forests. He sees farms and homesteads and gives them a wide berth. The young man traverses streams and fords swift flowing rivers. He climbs over rock formations and hikes rough escarpments. As the late afternoon sun begins to set on the horizon, Yuji camps on a mountain peak and views the pristine wilderness, he lays out his equipment and picks up a honing stone to sharpen his sword.

The next day, Yuji treks over the rough terrain and stops to adjust the duffle bag. He looks down and notices he's standing in the middle of a blueberry patch. Feeling a bit hungry, Yuji bends down to pick handfuls of berries to eat. To the far side, figures hidden by the forest carefully watch Yuji. A hunting party of Shoshone warriors observe the lone traveller from their wooded seclusion. Bear Claw, the leader of the group, stands with Eagle Feather, Two Knives, Thunder Cloud, Otter and other braves. Otter raises his bow to shoot an arrow at the unsuspecting traveller, but Bear Claw quickly stops him, "Hold! Do not shoot. He walks our land only seeking a path. We will not harm without cause." Otter gives a brash reply, "He walks our Tribe's land and takes our food. He has no right." Bear Claw gazes fatherly at the impetuous young warrior, "Our forests and rivers have many animals, birds, fish and berries. One man passing through will not remove our plenty." The others in the hunting party agree and support Bear Claw. Eagle Feather speaks up, "Bear Claw has spoken wise. Let the stranger pass untouched." Two Knives steps up, "Last night, I dreamed an eagle flying above a small fox. The eagle did not attack the little creature." The fellow hunters nod upon hearing such words. Eagle Feather turns to the others, "The sky bird is Bear Claw and the little fox is the stranger. If we attack - the Great Spirit will be angry with us. Bear Claw is right!" The hunting party heartily accept such insight and prepare to continue their expedition. The braves follow single file along the forest path. Bear Claw pauses momentarily to look back at the traveller, then he resumes his pace with the group. Otter also looks back at the stranger, his fingers brush the arrow feathers; suddenly, Otter turns and runs to catch up with the hunting party.

Yuji treks through a hollow in the woods with embankments on both sides. Up ahead, he notices flat rocks that jut out of the ground to create a dead end. As he walks, Yuji feels one of the leg straps is loose and he bends down to tie it secure. When he lifts his head - Yuji looks directly into the eyes of a large black timber wolf. The wolf snarls and bares its sharp fangs, the animal's saliva drips from its teeth, the hairs on its body becomes bristled. Yuji hears other sounds and turns around to see a pack of wolves surrounding him on all sides. The animals growl and snarl exposing their vicious teeth. In an instant, Yuji pulls his two sharp swords from the duffle bag - the polished steel blades gleam in the sunlight. In his right hand, he grips the long Katana and in his left hand is the short Ninjato sword. Yuji takes a fighting stance - swords ready for battle. The wolf pack leader, the Alpha male, confronts Yuji, snarling and snapping its jaws as it inches closer and closer. Around him the other wolves move in. With a loud snarl, the big wolf leaps to attack. Yuji steps forward and swings the long blade hard slicing open the Alpha wolf's neck. It falls yelping and dies. Then a timber wolf on his left attacks and Yuji stabs it with the Ninjato sword. A wolf behind him lunges and sinks its fangs into his Achilles tendon. Yuji twists his torso and kills it with the long sword. Suddenly, a wolf from the right runs and leaps toward Yuji's head. He blocks with his right arm, the wolf buries its fangs into his forearm. Instinctively, Ninja training kicks in and Yuji uses his left arm to plunge the short sword deep into the wolf's chest. It drops dead. Yuji does a quick turnabout to size up the situation - he sees four dead animals on the ground and eight more wolves circle to get closer. Yuji looks at his right arm which is loosing blood and he can only hobble because of the torn Achilles tendon on his left leg. The frenzied wolves snarl, growl and howl - thirsty for blood! Yuji looks at the stone outcrop yards away. The rock offers some form of defence - there he can protect his back from attack. The wolves creep in to lunge and bite at his feet and legs. Yuji frantically swings the two swords to fend off the animals. He hobbles and drags his left leg to get closer to the rocks. The wolves repeatedly snap their jaws at him - he fights them on all sides. Finally, Yuji reaches the stone outcrop and plants his back firmly against the flat granite. The stone is both a defence and a support for his body. Yuji leans back to catch his breath. He reaches into the duffle bag and brings out a bracket with sharp metal spikes and slips it over his right foot to create another weapon. He looks out to see the wolves run back and forth in front and to the sides. His eyes track the eight wolves - the two swords and the foot spike will only kill three - five more wolves can still attack. Yuji begins to feel weak from the loose of blood, his strength wanes, he's tired and breathes heavy. An outburst of snarls alert Yuji the wolves are closing in for the kill. The pack lunge in again and again to bite and grab his feet, arms and legs. Yuji bravely flails and kicks at the wolves. As he stabs a wolf on his left, the wolf on his right bites into Yuji's calf, its fangs sink deep into Yuji's flesh. He raises the long sword and drives the blade into the back of the wolf and kills it! Yuji lifts his head just as another wolf leaps and knocks him to the ground. In the tumble, the duffle bag slips off. The wolves converge and begin to bite and tear at his legs, torso, arms and head. Yuji rolls and uses his hands and arms to protect his face; but now his torso and legs are vulnerable. The wolves ferociously bite his body all over - Yuji fights for his life! Suddenly, GUN SHOTS! Bullets strike and kill four wolves, the other two remaining wolves yelp loud and run off. Yuji lays on his back with his clothes bloody and ripped - his legs, arms and body riddled with bites and torn flesh. With fading strength he looks up to see blurry figures loom over him. Yuji passes out!

Bear Claw, Eagle Feather, Two Knives, Thunder Cloud, Otter and the others stand over Yuji. Eagle Feather bends down to examine the damage - he looks at the wounds and cuts, bites are everywhere. He stands up and points to Yuji, "We must bring him to our camp or he will die." Otter bends over to peer at the stranger's face and motionless body. The young brave turns to Bear Claw and asks, "What Tribe does he belong to? He is not a white man." Two Knives speaks up, "His clothing is strange. He is not Pawnee, Sioux or Cheyenne." Thunder Cloud studies the stranger before them, "He is not Crow, Arapaho or Blackfoot." Otter looks at Bear Claw, "If he is not from the tribes we know - what tribe is he?" Bear Claw looks at Otter in silence, then gazes down at Yuji and turns his gaze to the hunting party, "The Healers in camp will help him. We must care for him until his strength returns." The leader motions to some braves and they find long branches to construct a litter to carry Yuji back to their camp. Bear Claw picks up the two swords, metal bracket and duffle bag. He gives the bag to Otter to carry and hands the two swords and bracket to Thunder Cloud. The braves carefully lift Yuji and place him into the sling. When Bear Claw sees Yuji is secure, he motions for the group to head back to camp. The Shoshone hunting party trek the path home - through soaring trees, past waterfalls, over lush meadows, and across rolling grassland. This time, instead of carrying an elk - they carry a human being.

CHAPTER FIFTEEN
The Shoshone Village

The Shoshone camp is picturesque and serene, nestled on the large bend of a wide gentle river. Eighty-nine tepees are spread out to form the Tribal village. Ample space lays between each dwelling for people and horses to manoeuvre. Smoke rises from many tepees as the women cook for the evening meal. The Chief's tepee stands in the centre, taller and much larger than the other dwellings. This is the place where the Indian leaders meet for Tribal Council. Bear Claw and the hunters stand on the crest of a grassy hill, the Shoshone village spread out before them. Thunder Cloud fires his rifle and waves his arm and shouts the customary signal. People at the edge of camp turn their heads in the direction of the gunshot. They hear the signal and see the braves on the hill. The excited villagers announce the news, "Bear Claw and the others are here." Another man shouts out, "The hunting party have returned." Word quickly travels through camp and everyone stirs to move and greet the hunting party. Men, women and children scurry past the Chief's tepee to welcome the returning braves. Out from the large tepee steps the Shoshone Chief Buffalo Sky, dressed in his buckskin outfit embroidered with beadwork and decorative metal. A feathered headdress adorns his braided snow white hair. Buffalo Sky stands noble and regal as he waits.

Bear Claw, Eagle Feather, Thunder Cloud, Two Knives, Otter and the other braves are greeted by the delighted villagers. Suddenly, their excitement turns to quiet wonder as they see the braves carry a strange person in the sling. The villagers walk with the hunting party, the people talking among themselves. Some inquisitive ones get close enough to peer in at the badly wounded stranger. By now, the hunting party are surrounded by the entire camp, everyone buzzing with curiosity about the man in the sling. Bear Claw and the returning warriors approach Chief Buffalo Sky's tepee. He awaits them with the Tribal Elders.

Buffalo Sky welcomes Bear Claw and the hunting party, "Your moccasins have carried you home. My heart is warm to see you and the braves again!" Bear Claw and the hunters stand respectful before their revered Chief. The seasoned hunter remarks, "There were no elk, sheep or bear on our hunt. We did find a strange man walking our lands!" Buffalo Sky looks at Bear Claw, "We will see this stranger." Bear Claw motions to the braves to bring the litter up for Buffalo Sky to see. The Chief and Tribal Elders come close for a better glimpse. Bear Claw points at Yuji, "This one showed great courage! He fought a pack of wolves by himself - killing many." Bear Claw's words catch Buffalo Sky's attention and the Chief lowers down to examine Yuji and notices the many injuries, "The wolf bites are deep and many!" Bear Claw speaks out, "He needs our Healers or he will die! This one is brave and has strong medicine." As Bear Claw and the hunting party stand before the Chief, many of the tribe's onlookers converse loudly among themselves about the stranger. Buffalo Sky looks around at his people and raises his hand high in the air, and the camp becomes quiet to hear his words, "Take him to the Healers' tepee. They will help him live. When he walks again, we will talk with him." Eagle Feather and Bear Claw smile at the Chief's decision. The hunting party turn and carry the litter past many dwellings before coming to the Healers' tepee. The villagers follow at a respectful distance. By this time, word of the events have reached the Healers. They emerge from their decorated tepee.

The hunting party bring the litter before the Healers as they stand at the entrance of their dwelling. Their Shoshone garb and markings identify them as Great Spirit Walkers. These are the ones to whom the Shoshone people bring their sick to be healed and restored. The Healers mix special plants, roots, herbs and flowers to make ointments, salves and compresses. Then the Shoshone Healers sing and chant to call on the Great Spirit. Bear Claw instructs the braves to gently set the litter down, and he speaks with the oldest Healer, Grey Bird. Next to the elderly man is a young Shoshone maiden called Bright Star, and beside her is a Shoshone woman known as Hair That Dances and a middle-aged brave called Burns With Smoke. Bear Claw points to Yuji,

"Your medicine can help this man to recover from his wounds." Grey Bird steps closer, bends down and stretches out his weathered hand to move aside Yuji's clothing to see the injuries. His eyebrows raise, "He is greatly wounded! We must get him inside. He will need our special medicine if he is to live." Grey Bird stands up and motions with his hand for the braves to bring Yuji into the Healers' tepee. As the braves carry the litter through the opening, Hair That Dances guides where to lay the wounded stranger. The braves gently lay him down on a knee-high platform covered with Buffalo hides. Burns With Smoke carefully cuts away and removes the bloodied clothing to reveal terrible bites, gashes and torn flesh. Grey Bird looks at Bear Claw, "We will care for him until his strength returns. If the Great Spirit calls for him - we have no medicine for that." Bear Claw nods as he glances over at Yuji's body with it's life-threatening injuries - the hunter understands. He turns and leaves through the tepee entrance, the other braves follow.

Grey Bird begins to amass various roots, herbs and plants. Hair That Dances pours water into a blacken kettle and sets it over the coals of a fire pit. Burns With Smoke starts to grind seeds, flower petals and coloured powders together in a gourd bowl. As the three Healers are busy, Bright Star stares at Yuji. The fire and the hot coals cast a glow upon Yuji's face. Bright Star has never seen someone like him before. Burns With Smoke finishes grinding and holds out the gourd bowl, Hair That Dances takes it and dumps the mixture into the kettle of water. Grey Bird brings over a thick bundle of herbs, roots and plants, and drops in the items. He takes a wooden ladle and stirs the kettle to mix everything together. Burns with Smoke gets up and comes over to stand beside the old man, "I will make the stranger ready and smear Buffalo grease over the cuts and wolf bites." Grey Bird turns to him, "Hair That Dances will place the poultice on his wounds and torn flesh. When he is covered with our tribe's medicine, we must ask the Great Spirit to walk with us. Only then can he be strong again." The elderly man watches as Burns With Smoke applies the Buffalo grease, and Hair That Dances covers Yuji's injuries and wounds with the healing poultice, then she lays some fur blankets over Yuji. Next, all four Healers sit on the tepee floor and begin to sing and chant tribal songs to call on the Great Spirit. Outside the Healers' tepee, a full moon bathes the village in luminous light, their singing carries across the grassy plains.

* * *

Night has settled over the Shoshone camp and the Chief and Elders have gathered for Tribal Council. The leaders sit cross-legged to form a large inner circle. The other warriors stand around the tepee's interior wall. Bear Claw, Eagle Feather, Thunder Cloud and Two Knives stand before Buffalo Sky and the Elders. Bear Claw tosses the black leather duffle bag into the centre of the circle. Buffalo Sky opens the bag and takes out the long and short sword and the metal bracket to examine them, then he passes the items around to the Elders. Next, the Chief lifts up the duffle bag and empties the contents onto the tepee floor. Out fall assorted leather pouches, different bundled clothes, tied scrolls, cloth bags, a knotted black rope, a black metal hook, black metal stars, a hollow reed, and a pouch of coins. The Chief passes these items to the Elders for their inspection. Buffalo Sky looks up at Bear Claw, "This stranger is unlike any we have ever met. When my eyes fell on him - I did not see a white man." An Elder remarks, "He must be an Indian from beyond our lands." Eagle Feather picks up the Katana sword and raises it high, "We saw him fight the wolves with his long knives. In his tribe, he must be a mighty warrior." Buffalo Sky rolls the pointed metal star with his fingertips, then he picks up the hollow reed and looks through it, "These are strange things before us. Things we have never seen - things our hands do not know." Bear Claw lowers down eye-level to the Chief, "When the stranger becomes strong, we will bring him to speak with our Chief and Elders. He will tell us about his tribe and lands." Buffalo Sky ponders a minute then stands to his feet and lifts his arms and looks around the tepee, "Until Bear Claw brings the stranger to us - we will hunt, fish and ride our horses after Buffalo." The Elders and the assembled warriors nod approval. The Chief signals and the hunting party and all the warriors leave the tepee. Only Buffalo Sky and the Elders remain.

CHAPTER SIXTEEN
Cutter and the Outlaws

The American Wild West attracts all kinds of people seeking its wide open spaces, fresh water, farmland and beautiful wilderness. Young and old venture forth to etch out a place for themselves. From railroad settlements, mining camps and frontier towns, to big ranches and small humble farms, the people work hard to make a new and better life.

Somewhere in the wilderness…

Cutter and his gang of outlaws sit around a roaring campfire. Cutter leans back against his saddle on the ground. The men smoke cigarettes and pass around a bottle of booze, some play cards within the flicker of the firelight, while others clean and polish their pistols and rifles. A rough-looking cowboy turns to Cutter, "Who we robbing next? That bank was a tough one!" The gang leader stares at the flames of the fire, "Farms! We gonna rob farmers. Take things easy for a while - til the next gold shipment by stage coach." Gang members close to him look at each other, sneer and grin. As the night presses on, some of the bandits try to get some shuteye. A few keep at their card game. Cutter stretches out his long legs, closes his eyes and repositions his cowboy hat to cover his face.

In the flats of a gentle valley, a farmer, his pretty young wife and their three youngsters are busy with chores. The oldest son chops wood and the two younger ones help carry the kindling to the house. The wife hangs up freshly washed clothes on the laundry line. Their playful spotted Collie suddenly turns and starts to bark at the far grove of trees. The farmer and his wife turn to see a group of men ride out from the cover of the woods. The young mom waves the children to her side. The farmer takes the wood axe and sets it on the ground against his leg. The nine outlaws gallop toward the huddled family. A number of yards away, the group splits up, three ride to the left, three riders go to the right, while Cutter and two men stop in front. The young family are trapped in the middle. The farmer and his wife glance around at the riders - the men are dusty and dirty with the look of meanness etched into their scruffy unshaved faces. Cutter looks around at the farmhouse, barn and water well. The farmer takes a step forward, "You men can water your horses and you're welcome to any food we have." The farmer looks about and notices the men leer at his attractive young wife. Cutter stiffens his legs in the stirrups and stands tall and gives the farmer a mean stare, "Who are you to tell us what we can and cannot do? We aim to do as we please." The farmer makes eye contact with his frightened wife and scared children, then he looks up at the gang leader, "I meant no disrespect. I was just being hospitable." The man on the horse beside Cutter speaks out, "You're trying to be (strutters) hos-pit - hosp-it." The gang leader frowns and gives the man a glaring stare. Cutter speaks out, "Hospitable." The farmer smiles, "Yes Sir, that's right! Just wantin' to be neighbourly." Some of the riders snicker loud as they look at the young lady. One outlaw remarks, "We like neighbourly...neighbourly means sharing (he eyes the wife) and we like sharing." The farmer instinctively moves to stand in front of his pretty wife and raises the axe from his side, "You men are more than welcome to food and water. After that, I'll be seeing you leave." The riders chuckle and snicker. A man yells, "What if we don't want to leave. Who's gonna stop us all - you?" The farmer stands straight and tall, "I will if I have to!" The exchange makes all the bandits break out laughing, some mock, some jest, and some have icy stares. The gang leader moves his horse out from the others and brings his mount a couple feet in front of the farmer and stares at him, "Sod buster, I like your grit. Yes Sir, I truly do." Cutter spins his pistol chamber, "But this here tells me we can do whatever we want!" The riders let out loud yahoos and shoot their guns in the air. The farmer with a sad face, turns to his trembling wife with tears running down her face - and urgently pleads, "Run! Run!" The farmer turns back to the gang leader, and Cutter points his gun and shoots the farmer square in the chest. The farmer drops dead to the ground. The wife and frightened children watch in horror - instinctively they flee to the farmhouse. The young mother reaches the porch and frantically waves to her children, "Run!Hurry - Run!" The riders open fire and shoot the children in the back. The terrified mother watches in horror as her three children tumble to the ground like discarded rag dolls, their lifeless bodies lay in the dirt. The family dog barks angrily at the intruders, and an outlaw aims his pistol and shoots the dog dead. The young woman lifts her eyes off her dead children and sees the men dismount and slowly walk toward her. Terror comes over her, she instantly knows her fate at the hands of these ruthless men. She races inside and bolts the heavy door and lays a thick wood beam across its back. Then she quickly goes to the two windows and locks the strong wood shutters. The badmen are now on the porch, some try to force open the door but no success, others try the windows but they're are sealed shut. The young lady can hear the sound of boots and spurs going across the wood porch. She turns her head to the glass frame that holds their family portrait. It's more precious than ever and she reaches out and brings it to her bosom. Outside on the porch, the bandits are frustrated and angry at being thwarted by a young woman. Cutter strides up with the axe in hand and tosses it to a man in front of the door, "You boys really need to think more!" Cutter motions for the man to begin chopping. The others start to holler and yell with excitement! Inside the house, the young lady shutters as she hears the axe chip away at the thick wood door. She holds the cherished photo and collects all the kerosene lamps in the house. The young wife goes into her bedroom and takes a lingering look at her husband's clothes, her dresses, her fancy collectables, her daughter's dolly, and her youngest son's teddy bear. She opens the lamps and throws kerosene on the bedroom door, the wood floorboards, the walls, the furniture, and the mattress. She garbs a box of matches, her fingers tremble as she tries to strike a flame - it goes out - she lights another and it goes out. She strikes the third match and it burns bright. The young woman lifts her head as she hears the axe break through the door. The bandits kick-in and bust down the big door and barge into the interior. She puts the lit match against the kerosene on the door, then she drops the burning match on the floor. Then she goes and lays down on her bed and presses the family photo against her heart. In seconds, flames engulf the bedroom, everything becomes ablaze - the bedroom door, the walls, the floor and the furniture on fire. The badmen reach the burning bedroom door but a wall of flames bar their access. The heat is intense and the men back off. Cutter pushes his way through to the front and peers through the flames and meets the haunting eyes of the young woman. She lays serene as she holds the family picture. Suddenly, the fire reaches her bed and she disappears in a shroud of flames. Now, the entire bedroom is an inferno and fire quickly spreads throughout the farmhouse. The nine riders hack and cough as they flee the burning smoke-filled building. They race to their horses and mount up. Cutter looks at his men, "Let's go boys! Nothing here for us. Let's ride!" The group of heartless outlaws gallop away, riding past the dead bodies of the farmer and his three young children laying in the dirt - the wood farmhouse burning in the background.

CHAPTER SEVENTEEN

The Jacobs Farm

Abner Josiah Jacobs and his wife Mary Jacobs sit at a large kitchen table for a late afternoon meal with their two sons, Edison (22), and the youngest, Henry (19). Mrs Jacobs has prepared a hearty supper. The oldest sons, Levi (26) and Daniel (23), are tending livestock in the barn. The father looks over to his youngest, "Henry, go call your brothers for supper! (Smiles to his wife) We sure don't want your mother's fine cooking to get cold." Henry promptly gets up, "Yes Sir Pa! Right away." Henry scurries across the wide front porch and jumps off into the dirt yard. He high-tails it to the big wood structure and stands outside the barn doors and calls to his brothers, "Levi. Daniel. Come on for supper! Pa says right away too." Henry happily nods, pleased that he delivered the message, turns and heads back to the large farmhouse. He runs and takes a flying leap onto the porch and quickly enters the house. Inside the barn, Levi holds a baby calf that has lost its mother and needs to be nursed. He has a glass bottle of milk in his hand. Daniel stands next to him and reaches out to brush the calf's forehead, "Will the calf manage until we're back from supper?" His older brother looks at him, "You go on ahead - tell mom I'm sorry for missing her nice supper, but this little calf needs help." Daniel lifts his arm, smiles and messes Levi's hair, "Okay, I'll tell her, and just so you know, I'm eating yours too!" Levi grins and raises his boot to give a playful kick, but Daniel is too fast and he's out of the barn for the house. Levi glances down at the little calf in his arms and whispers, "We didn't need him anyways." Levi finds a wood bench and sits down and cuddles the calf and feeds it the bottle.

On a hilltop overlooking the Jacobs farm, Cutter and his gang sit on their horses. The men survey the large farmhouse, big barn, the stone wall, and the corral of horses. Cutter stands tall in his stirrups and leans out so him men can see him, "Boys, looks like easy pickings' - and all ours for the takin'." The riders sneer - their faces have gloating smiles.

Abner and Mary Jacobs and their sons, Edison, Henry and Daniel, finish up their family meal. Mrs. Jacobs rises and prepares a plate of food and covers it with a checkered cloth and hands it to Daniel, "Daniel, you take this plate of supper to Levi. He needs food just as much as that little calf." Her son promptly stands and takes the plate from his mom, "Yes Ma'am! I'll be as fast as a Jackrabbit." Daniel carefully carries the plate, opens and closes the front door on his way. Outside, he steps off the porch and begins to walk to the barn. Halfway between the house and the barn, he hears the neigh of horses and looks around. Daniel sees nine riders coming down the grassy slope toward the farm. He yells loudly, "Pa! Pa! Riders are coming. Riders are coming." He turns and dashes to the barn, quickly enters and shuts the doors behind him. Abner swiftly goes to the front door to look outside - he sees nine cowboys riding hard toward the house. The father closes and bolts the door secure. Abner dashes to the wall cabinet and swings open the double doors - inside the cabinet are Winchester rifles, shotguns, pistols, boxes of ammo, and sticks of dynamite. He turns around and yells, "Ma. Edison. Henry - grab a gun and ammo - get ready for shooting!" Mrs. Jacobs and her sons come over and each grab a gun and a box of ammo. Henry and his mom go to the kitchen window, and Edison stations himself at the parlour window. Abner with Winchester in hand, unbolts and opens the front door just enough to stick his head out. He sees the riders stop some distance out from the house. The gang of bandits aim their rifles and pistols at the farmhouse. Cutter stretches up in the saddle, "You folks in there better come out if you know what's good! No sense hiding and making it difficult and all." Mr Jacobs cracks the door open and shouts a warning, "You men are trespassing. You best leave while you can!" Abner's remark angers Cutter and he fires a bullet that hits the door - Abner quickly shuts the door and locks it. Cutter reins his horse in a tight circle and faces the farmhouse, "We're here to take your farm - and we'll kill anyone who tries to stop us!" Hearing those words, Abner, Mary, Edison and Henry, break window glass and aim the rifles at the riders. The outlaws see four rifles pointed at them. The gang becomes uneasy. An outlaw speaks up, "Boss, I think this farm isn't worth the trouble." Cutter leans over and swats the man across the face, "The problem is you try to think. Don't! Leave the thinkin' to me - that's my job. We're taking this farm, there's lots here for us. Come on boys!" The riders start to fire their guns at the farmhouse, bullets hit the walls, door and windows. They turn their horses toward the stone fence and ditch for cover. Abner and his family open fire blasting away - bullets hit three of the gang knocking them off their horses. One is shot in the chest, another struck in the back, and one wounded in the shoulder. From inside the barn, Levi and Daniel watch the commotion from between the barn doors. Levi motions to Daniel, "The tool box has a rifle and ammo!" Daniel hustles to the tool box and gets the rifle and ammo. Returning back, he tosses the gun and box of bullets to Levi, "You use it - you're a better shot." Daniel grabs a nearby pitchfork and shakes it, "If they get close, I'll use this." A round of gunfire alert their attention and they peek out the doors to see what's happening.

The gang of outlaws are hunkered down behind the stone fence and their horses are tied at the ditch. Cutter lifts his head and looks at the two bandits laying dead in the dust, then he glances at the man with the wounded shoulder who can't shot no more. Cutter looks over at a couple men close by and orders, "You two sneak over to the barn, try to get behind the house." The two men nod and the gang commence to shoot guns at the farmhouse while the two bandits duck low along the wood fence to the barn. The duo manage to get a hundred feet from the barn. Levi and Daniel spot the two outlaws sneaking to the barn and the two brothers hurry to the barn side door. Levi cocks the Winchester to chamber a round and looks at Daniel, "When I tell you - open the side door so I can get a shot off. We'll surprise them good!" Daniel nods and puts his hand on the door latch and waits for the signal. Levi takes a deep breath and nods, "Okay - Now!" Daniel pulls the side door open and Levi leans out to aim. The two bandits slinking along the fence are surprised and caught off guard. The two men aim their guns but Levi fires the rifle and kills the man in front. His partner unloads his pistol as he scoots back along the fence. Levi ducks inside as slugs take out chunks of the door and barn siding. The survivor works his way back to the gang. When Cutter sees the man return he gets mad, "What went wrong over there?" The man is shaken and angry, "Someone in the barn had a gun. Morgan's dead!" Cutter swats the fence with his hat in seething anger, "Two killed. Riley can't shoot.

Now Morgan's dead!"

At the house, Edison and Henry guard the parlour window, Abner and Mary are at the kitchen window. Edison strains to look outside and remarks, "Pa! Pa! What's going on? What are they doing?" Mr. Jacobs peers out the kitchen window and looks at his two sons, "They're hold up at the fence - likely figuring a way to get in here." In the momentary lull, the family check their rifles and reload ammunition. Henry pipes up, "We got three of them didn't we Pa? I saw three go down." The father replies, "Two are dead. We just wounded the other." Edison steps away from the window and looks at his parents, "I heard gunfire at the barn." Mrs. Jacobs gives Abner a worried look and reaches out to clasp her husband's arm, "What about Levi and Daniel?" Abner places his hand on her shoulder with firm assurance, "The lads will be fine. Levi knows about the rifle I keep in the tool box. They're both great shots." Mary relaxes a bit, "You're right! Our lads are good with a gun." Abner gives his wife a smile and a gentle squeeze. Mary nods her head and manages a smile. Abner chambers another round and looks out the window.

The gang is spread out along the stone wall with guns in hand - unsettled and antsy. One bandit asks the leader, "What are we gonna do boss?" Cutter makes a contorted face and replies, "Just let me think! - they got four rifles in the house and a gun in the barn. Five of them against five of us. (Laughs) We can storm the barn - only one gun there." The gang members agree and someone remarks, "Just give the word boss." The leader nods and all the outlaws get ready to rush the barn. Cutter signals and the gang members hunch their way toward the structure. Abner becomes alarmed as he spots the bandits heading toward the barn and notifies his family, "We got to help Levi and Daniel - they're going for the barn!" Edison and Henry rush over to their father, "Henry and I can run to the barn. Our extra guns will help!" Mary Jacobs puts a hand on each son's shoulder, "No! That's too dangerous. You both stay put." Mr. Jacobs looks at Mary and the two lads, "Edison, You and Henry and your mom pin them down. I'll take another rifle to the barn." They all exchanges glances and nod agreement. Mary puts her hand against her husband's face, "Abner, be careful!" He gives a firm smile and rushes to the cabinet to get another rifle. He goes by the front door and unlocks it, "Lay down lots of fire! Keep 'em busy so I can reach the barn (Abner cracks the front door open), "Okay. Now!" Edison, Henry and mom open rapid fire at the gang of robbers. Abner dashes out the door and heads full speed for the barn. The riders see Abner run for the barn and begin to open fire on him. Bullets whiz all around him - slugs hit the house, porch and posts. The gunfire from the farmhouse is fast and relentless. Edison hits one of the bandits in the arm. The hot lead makes the men duck for cover. As Abner gets inside the barn, Levi and Daniel are surprised and relieved to see their father. Abner tosses the spare rifle to Daniel, who catches it and checks the weapon and cocks the lever for action. Levi eyes his father, "Sure good to see you Pa!" The father looks at the two, "They were fixing to rush the barn. Too many for you (lifts his rifle) We just evened the odds." Then, Abner, Levi and Daniel go to the side of the barn and point their gun barrels out through the opening in the boards.

Cutter raises up his head to take stock of the situation. He sees three rifles sticking out from windows at the farmhouse, then he looks over to see three gun barrels pointing out from the barn. The outlaw flops back down and grumbles, "I don't like being pinned down like this!" One man exclaims, "Look! Now they got guns at the barn just like the house." Cutter jabs his finger in the man's face, "Shut up! Just shut up!" Cutter looks at his gang, lifts his head to take another look at the house and the barn, and barks, "Make a run for the horses, boys! We'll go some place else." The outlaws skedaddle for their horses and quickly mount up and ride off.

Mr. Jacobs sees the gang take off and turns to his lads, "They're leaving. High-tailing it out of here!" Daniel exclaims in excitement, "We beat them Pa! We scared them off." Levi swings open the barn doors, and all three step out into the barnyard. The front door of the farmhouse opens and Edison, Henry and Mrs. Jacobs walk out onto the porch. They all watch the riders disappear out of sight. Both groups meet and hug each other with big smiles and cheers! Edison chimes, "We sure showed them - didn't we!" The mother wraps her arm around Edison, "We sure did son! We sure did." As the four lads look in the direction the outlaws rode off in, Mr. and Mrs. Jacobs hug and kiss each other. Young Henry looks at his big brother, "What happens if they come back?" His three brothers look at him and Levi slaps Henry's back, "We'll take care of them. We'll shoot them all!" The mother comes over to her sons, "Evil men like that get what's coming to them." Levi tilts his head and gives his mom an inquisitive expression, "All this shooting has made me hungry - is there any more supper?" Mary Jacobs grins, shakes her head and waves Levi to go inside. Abner, Edison and Henry all burst out laughing. They all turn and ascend the steps of the wide porch, go inside and close the door. A couple minutes pass and the front door opens and Abner sticks his head for one last look around. He scans the horizon. Nothing. Abner with a confident smile, closes and bolts the door.

CHAPTER EIGHTEEN

Healer's Tepee

Bright Star sits beside Yuji as her eyes trace the features of his face. Hair That Dances comes up to stand on the other side. The women exchange glances. The older woman comments, "He's not like Indians we know. That is what the camp is saying." Bright Star tilts her head as she continues to study Yuji and replies with a curious tone, "Does he have family? Brothers? Sisters? Where does he come from?" Hair that Dances lifts the fur blanket to inspect his wounds. She looks at the young maiden, "Grey Bird says he will be strong in three moons. We must wait until his tongue knows to speak again." Bright Star gets up from her position and firmly remarks, "I will guard and watch over him with my eyes." Hair That Dances teases, "It is good for young eyes to watch over such a young warrior." Bright Star blushes. Hair That Dances walks to a ledge and grabs a small medicine pouch, "I must take some healing roots to Foxtail - their little girl is not well." The woman opens the tepee flap and leaves as Bright Star resumes her vigil over Yuji. Over the next three moons, the Healers keep giving their Tribe's special medicine to Yuji. Grey Bird and Burns With Smoke prepare soothing healing ointments, and Hair That Dances applies fresh dressing to the many wounds. During the evenings, the Healers sing and chant calling upon the Great Spirit. They take note of the young stranger's progress. At night during sleep, Grey Bird closely observes as Yuji tosses and turns as he sweats and repeatedly mumbles. One morning, the fever breaks and Yuji opens his eyes. Gradually, he becomes better and his health and strength return. The young man can sit up on his own, and over the succeeding days he begins to stand - and days later, Yuji walks. At night when Yuji peacefully sleeps, Bright Star tenderly watches him.

* * *

It is a warm day with a gentle breeze when Yuji comes out of the Healers' tepee to set foot outside. He stands and takes a deep breath to fill his lungs, beside him stand Grey Bird, Smoke That Burns, Hair That Dances and Bright Star. High above in the sky, a magnificent eagle soars overhead and cries out! Yuji and the Healers look up and Grey Bird comments, "The sky bird is a good sign!" Yuji lowers his eyes and looks around the Shoshone camp that's busy with the routines of daily life. Indian women carry firewood, children run and play, braves lead horses around, old men sit outside their tepees, and young maidens work and prepare leather skins. Five tepees away, Bear Claw and a group of braves turn their attention to Yuji and the Healers, and begin to walk toward them. The group walk up and Bear Claw scans Yuji from head to toe, then he looks at the Healers, "The Great Spirit has returned his strength. The stranger looks better!" Grey Bird muses, "After much medicine, chanting and singing - he will walk in moccasins again." Bear Claw turns and waves to a brave in the back of the group. The young brave brings up the black leather duffle bag and hands it to Bear Claw. The veteran warrior lifts the bag and holds it out. Yuji with an expression of appreciation, nods and takes the duffle bag and sets it down beside him. Yuji looks at Bear Claw and the group of braves - then he bows low before them. Bear Claw watches Yuji with curiosity and puzzlement as he's never encountered such a new and strange gesture. Bear Claw turns to Grey Bird, "In three fires, Buffalo Sky and the Elders will speak with the stranger." Grey Bird glances over at Yuji and replies, "He is strong now. His moccasins will carry him to the Council Fire." Bear Claw nods and he and the braves leave. Grey Bird, the Healers and Yuji go inside the decorated tepee.

CHAPTER NINETEEN
Yuji At The Tribal Council

The evening of the Tribal Council, Yuji is dressed in Shoshone garb and stands still. As the Healers chant, Grey Bird uses an eagle feather to wave smoke over him. Bear Claw and Thunder Cloud step into the tepee and Grey Bird remarks, "He is ready!" Bear Claw approaches Yuji to check his Indian clothing - everything is in order and he's pleased. Grey Bird takes Bear Claw aside and whispers into the warrior's ear - Bear Claw turns and gives Yuji a probing gaze. The warrior leader exclaims, "This evening, our people will hear his tongue and learn of him." Bear Claw gestures for Yuji to follow him and the three men step outside. They walk past many tepees and the villagers watch as they arrive at the Chief's dwelling. Inside the large central tepee, Buffalo Sky, the Elders and the warriors have gathered for the Tribal Council. The men talk with keen anticipation! Bear Claw, Thunder Cloud and Yuji step through the door flap and remain standing. All conversations stop, everyone looks at them. Buffalo Sky raises his hand high and gazes around to address the assembled warriors, "Tonight, the stranger will speak at our Council Fire. We will learn of him and his people." Bear Claw leads Yuji to stand before the Chief and Elders. He sits down cross-legged and motions Yuji to sit down also. Bear Claw eyes the Chief and the Elders, and remarks, "I have Big Medicine to tell - Grey Bird said the stranger spoke Shoshone words during the fever!" Buffalo Sky, the Elders and all the warriors are shocked and surprised. Everyone turns their gaze to Yuji. The Chief watches Yuji for a couple of moments then speaks, "The stranger speaks the white man's tongue. Jumping Horse will talk with him so we can learn." The Chief waves his arm to beckon Jumping Horse who comes and sits down beside Yuji. Buffalo Sky leans toward Jumping Horse, "Ask who he is? - And where is his tribe?" Jumping Horse turns to face Yuji and opens his mouth in English, "Tell us about yourself? Where do you come from? Who are your people?" Yuji's eyes light up at hearing English. He looks at Jumping Horse, "I was five years old when a white man, Blake Connors, found me wandering alone in the brush. I lived at the Stage Coach Station in Emerson, and looked after the horses." Jumping Horse translates what Yuji said and The Chief, Elders and all the braves listen intently. Then Jumping Horse asks Yuji, "Where is your family? Where are your people?" Yuji replies, "All I remember is getting separated from my mother and big sister. I remember some Indian words they spoke." Jumping Horse translates again and Buffalo Sky asks, "What Indian words can he speak?" Jumping Horse turns to question Yuji, "Speak the Indian words you know." Yuji opens his mouth slightly and pauses - he glances around at all the warriors - then he blurts out, "Bia'- Ape'- Sadee'- Bambi - Baa'." Buffalo Sky, the Elders and everyone are totally stunned. The men turn to each other in shock, an Elder comments, "He speaks our tongue - Shoshone!" All the men in the tepee are spell-bound, their eyes riveted on Yuji. The Chief motions to Jumping Horse, "Ask how he became lost?" The brave relays the question, "How did you get lost? Do you remember?" Yuji lowers his eyes and stares at the flickering flames of the fire and begins to speak, Jumping Horse translates each line Yuji utters, "Bad men attacked our village. My mother, sister and I ran to hide in the tall grass. Mother told me don't make a sound. The bad men found us - so we ran as fast as we could through the tall grass. They were ahead but I could not keep up. Suddenly, they were gone! I could not see them anymore, so I hid in the grass a long time and stayed quiet. Then, I wandered for a long time. - Blake Connors found me by a river bank, picked me up and carried me to town. There, I lived in the big horse barn." The entire tepee is hushed and silent - everyone transfixed by Yuji's story. Jumping Horse makes eye contact with Buffalo Sky, then asks, "How did you come to us from the white man?" Yuji turns toward Jumping Horse and replies, "When I was twelve years old, a Japanese man named Takeshi hired me as farm help. But he became as a father to me. Over the years, I learned his Japanese ways and language. Later, Takeshi taught me his ancient Ninja skills." As Jumping horse translates - everyone is fascinated. The Chief motions to Jumping Horse, "What is Ninja?" The Shoshone interpreter asks Yuji, "The Chief and Elders want to know - what is Ninja?" Yuji scans the tepee. All eyes are on him, Yuji replies, "Ninja is from a land very far away called Japan. You travel many days on a large boat over a great water called the ocean. Ninja skills were born in the Iga Mountains. Ninja is called the Secret Way!" Jumping Horse translates Yuji's account and all the men are enthralled. Buffalo Sky requests Jumping Horse enquire of the stranger, "Tell us of Ninja?" As he speaks and Jumping Horse translates into Shoshone, Yuji tells the history of the Ninja Clans that lived in the Iga Mountains of Japan. The Ninja developed their fighting skills and guarded their Ninja knowledge and secrets for generations. A mighty Warlord made a surprise attack on their villages. Four thousand Ninja fought against forty thousand soldiers. Overpowered and greatly outnumbers, the remaining Ninja escaped and scattered across the country taking their special knowledge with them to keep it secret. The Japanese man, Takeshi, was the last of his Ninja Clan. He searched for someone to pass on his Ninja skills. Takeshi found me and trained me to become a Ninja! Yuji turns to look at the Chief and Elders, then looks at Jumping Horse, "When I learned all he taught - Takeshi made me a Ninja Master, and gave me all his Ninja possessions, weapons and ancient scrolls." The entire tepee sits in a long hushed silence, then an Elder stands up and comes over to Yuji and closely examines his facial features and appearance. The Elder turns about for all in the tepee to see and hear, "His Shoshone tongue has been buried living in the white man's town. My heart tells me he is Shoshone. His moccasins have found their way home to his people." Buffalo Sky stands up, smiles broadly and lifts his arms and proclaims, "We must celebrate and dance - a lost Shoshone boy has returned to us - a strong young man!" Everyone stands. The Chief, Elders and assembled warriors yell Shoshone victory cries of celebration! Yuji looks about as he stands still and silent.

CHAPTER TWENTY
Shoshone Camp Celebration

A huge bonfire lights up the night sky. All the Shoshone, both young and old, gather to celebrate Yuji's return. The drums beat, the singers chant, and the people dance - there is food, fun and festivity all about. The children play games and enjoy treats. Young warriors dance with young maidens, and Buffalo Sky and the Elders watch the special event with gladness. Yuji stands next to Jumping Horse, Bear Claw and Eagle Feather. The young man looks out at the celebration and remarks, "I have never been treated like this by so many!" Jumping Horse smiles and replies, "You were lost little brother, now, you are among your people." As the night goes on, many villagers come up to Yuji to welcome him - old folks, children, warriors, maidens, young braves, and Elders. Yuji politely smiles and nods as the people show their support and acceptance.

The following day, Yuji sits with Bear Claw, Thunder Cloud and Jumping Horse as they begin to teach him Shoshone words and customs. Bear Claw would point to an object and speak the Shoshone word and Yuji would attempt the pronunciation. Yuji would repeat each word until Bear Claw would grin satisfaction. Thunder Cloud would take Yuji around the village to identify things and Yuji would try to sound out the word as Bear Claw and Jumping Horse encouraged him.

Early one morning, Bear Claw rises and exits the tepee and walks through the village until he abruptly stops and watches transfixed. In the rays of the morning sun - Yuji practices his swordsmanship handling the Katana blade with amazing moves of speed, agility and skill. The expression on Bear Claw's face shows that he's greatly impressed and he quietly moves on not to disturb Yuji's Ninja discipline.

Life in the Shoshone camp is pleasant and peaceful, and Yuji becomes well-adjusted to the daily routines. It is on his walks about the village that Yuji begins to notice Bright Star. One afternoon, they happen to be near one another as people watch the children play a game. It is on that occasion that Yuji and Bright Star exchange interested glances and shy smiles. One morning, Bright Star strolls along the riverbank and stops to admire some water Lillies - Yuji notices and wades into the river and reaches his hand into the water to pick out a beautiful flower from the surface. He climbs out of the river and comes up to Bright Star and offers her the lovely flower. Bright Star takes the Lilly and gives Yuji a sweet smile. From that day onward, the villagers would often see the young man and the young maiden walking together. One day, Eagle Feather and Gold Flower stand outside their tepee and see Bright Star and Yuji together. Eagle Feather has a proud smile.

CHAPTER TWENTY-ONE
Chief And Elders Want To See Ninja?

Yuji sits with Chief Buffalo Sky and the Elders; Bear Claw, Thunder Cloud, Eagle Feather, Two Knives, and Jumping Horse are also present. Jumping Horse turns to Yuji to ask, "The Chief and Elders want to see Ninja" Yuji replies, "I can show them and the whole camp tomorrow." Jumping Horse relays the message and Buffalo Sky and the others briefly talk; when they finish - The Chief looks at Jumping Horse and nods approval. Jumping Horse informs Yuji, "The whole village will be there." Yuji glances around at the Chief and others and politely smiles and nods to them, "Ask the Chief to pick out your ten best warriors to fight me." Jumping Horse speaks Yuji's request and Buffalo Sky and the other men look oddly at Yuji. The Chief turns to Jumping Horse, "Tell him there is great danger in what he asks! Does he know this?" Jumping Horse translates the Chief's question and Yuji replies, "Make sure you select your strongest fighters. Tomorrow, you will see what my Master, Takeshi, taught me." Hearing from Jumping Horse, all eyes fix on Yuji - Buffalo Sky glances around the gathered men - then nods agreement. Yuji stands to his feet and bows respectfully to the Chief and the Elders, then exits the tepee. After Yuji has gone - Buffalo Sky turns to Bear Claw with an inquisitive look and asks in all seriousness, "What he asks is very strange. Did he hit his head fighting the wolves?" Bear Claw responds with a puzzled grin, "No. He did not injure his head - I also do not understand what he asks?!" Chief Buffalo Sky dismisses the assembly and everyone leaves. Alone in the large tepee, Buffalo Sky stares quietly at the fire.

The next day, the entire camp is assembled, all the villagers from the youngest to the oldest watch with interest and excitement. Ten of the best and most capable Shoshone warriors stand ready; armed with knives, tomahawks, war clubs and spears. Buffalo Sky and the Tribe's Elders watch from their vantage point. Yuji emerges from his tepee dressed in his Ninja outfit and walks to the large clear area and stands in the middle. He looks at Jumping Horse, "Tell them to attack me with their weapons." Jumping Horse shouts out the instructions. The villagers are a buzz at hearing such words. Yuji nods to Jumping Horse and the brave shouts aloud, "Attack!" The warriors yell war cries and each with weapon in hand, begin to move and circle the lone defender. Yuji looks around and assesses each attacker's weapon and position. He takes a Ninja battle stance. All eyes are glued to the impending action. Suddenly, one of the bigger braves runs at him and lunges with a knife. Yuji grabs the brave's arm and throws him high in the air to land head first in the dirt. Another warrior attacks with a raised tomahawk. Yuji blocks the tomahawk swing, grabs the man's arms, rolls backward and catapults him through the air to land hard yards away. Thud! Buffalo Sky, the Elders and Bear Claw and warriors are amazed at Yuji's speed and agility. Yuji pivots and scans about just as two braves attack at the same time, one from the front, the other from the back. Yuji quickly spins and kicks one attacker to knock him out; then Yuji turns and pummels the other attacker with a barrage of rapid blows that immobilize him - Yuji takes the knife from his hand and tosses it away. By now, the entire camp are wide-eyed and totally captivated. The six remaining warriors glance at each other and attack in a rage with loud shouts and war cries. Bright Star is worried that Yuji may become harmed. Eagle Feather and Gold Flower see her concern. As the six braves launch their attack, one brave throws a spear at Yuji who catches the spear by the shaft, twirls it to strike another brave unconscious. One brave wildly swings his war clubs and Yuji ducks and dodges the assault. Yuji moves in to block and deliver punches to drop the brave to the ground. The last three warriors lunge toward the lone fighter. Yuji jumps high to kick and knock out two braves! He lands and puts the last brave in a sleeper hold until the warrior stops struggling and passes out. Yuji lets him fall to the ground. Yuji stands alone and victorious in the middle of the battle area; the ten braves are beaten, bruised and defeated, their weapons lay in the dirt. Buffalo Sky, the Elders, Bear Claw, Thunder Cloud, Two Knives and Jumping Horse are all stunned and excited after witnessing such an incredible fight. The Chief looks at Jumping Horse, "Bring him before us." The brave fetches Yuji and brings him in front of Buffalo Sky. The Chief motions to Jumping Horse, "Ask if he will teach our warriors to fight his way?" Jumping Horse conveys the Chief's request and Yuji bows low before the Chief and Tribe's leaders, "Shoshone warriors saved my life! Tell the Chief and Elders that I will pick Shoshone braves to train as Ninja." Jumping Horse smiles and gladly translates Yuji reply. Hearing Yuji's answer, Buffalo Sky steps forward and looks into the young man's eyes, the Chief slowly speaks, "N - in - ja! Nin - ja! Ninja!" Yuji bows, smiles and replies. "Aho! Ninja." At that moment, Bear Claw reaches into his beaded buckskin tunic and brings out a large black eagle feather and offers it to Yuji. Yuji takes the black feather and admires its beauty and quality. Jumping Horse leans near Yuji and comments, "Bear Claw has greatly honoured you! The Black Feather is only given to our very best warrior." Yuji exchanges eye contact with Bear Claw and Yuji bows very low before him. Yuji remarks, "Osereirimasu! My highest thanks to you." Yuji turns and walks away and returns to his tepee. As he passes by the villagers, they stare at him in awe and wonder.

CHAPTER TWENTY-TWO
Young Romance

It's a beautiful summer day with blue skies and puffy white clouds. Bright Star and Yuji walk by the river appreciating some uninterrupted moments together. Yuji picks a pretty flower and gives it to Bright Star. She brings the flower close and smells its fragrant scent and looks at Yuji with a delighted smile. Then they continue to walk side by side along the riverbank. Later in camp as Bright Star lifts a water jug, Yuji comes up and takes the water jug and carries it for her. And during chores and activities in the village, Yuji looks over at Bright Star whenever he can. Because of Shoshone rules between young braves and young maidens, Bright Star and Yuji can only give one another shy smiles whenever they pass each other. As Bright Star sits with the other young maidens, she watches him with reserved affection. On one afternoon, Yuji approaches Bright Star and stands before her and holds out a lovely beaded necklace. Bright Star's eyes widen at seeing the fine decorative piece. He looks at her, nods and extends the necklace toward her. She clasps the pretty item and puts it over her head to wear. Bright Star's delight is very apparent and she beams with happiness. After some weeks have passed, Yuji eats the evening meal with Eagle Feather, Gold Flower and Bright Star. Gold Flower knows Yuji is hungry and gives him generous portions. As he devours his food, Eagle Feather, Gold Flower and Bright Star grin.

CHAPTER TWENTY-THREE

Shoshone Ninja Trained And Tested

Only the sound of forest birds fill the morning air, everything else in the Shoshone camp is quiet. All able Shoshone braves stand in the open ground with space between each of them, Otter is also there. Around them the entire camp have gathered to observe this new thing brought to their tribe. Yuji stands before the warriors and walks past each one to observe his physical condition, muscle tone, and the manner he presents himself. Buffalo Sky, Bear Claw, Thunder Cloud, Eagle Feather, Two Knives, and the Elders watch from the side. The Shoshone braves stand with anticipation, their physical bodies strong and muscular, their stance tall and proud, ready to be selected to honour their tribe. Some are so filled with nervous energy they can only breathe short shallow breaths, while others stand calm and still. The villagers that ring the Tribe's candidates remain quiet, no one saying anything, no one talks, everyone wants to pay close attention to which brave will be selected. Yuji moves through the braves and makes his selection by looking into the candidate's eyes and tapping their shoulder. Yuji walks back to his central spot and slowly scans the group of young men as he ponders and thinks - then Yuji steps out and comes up to stand in front of Otter. Yuji looks directly into Otter's eyes and studies the young man, then Yuji reaches out his hand and taps Otter on the shoulder. Yuji returns to his position content he has found ten suitable braves for Shoshone Ninja training. Yuji smiles and looks over to Jumping Horse and nods success. Jumping Horse lifts his voice loud and clear for all to hear, "If your shoulder was touched - stay - all others must leave." The braves who did not have their shoulder tapped, move out in all directions and join the circle of onlookers. Yuji and the entire camp look upon the ten braves that stand intersperse in the open ground. The successful braves exchange eye contact with one another, then look at Yuji who smiles at them. Jumping Horse makes the announcement, "These are the braves to be trained by Yuji to become Shoshone Ninja warriors!" The Chief, Elders, and all the Shoshone people shout out cries of Celebration!

The Shoshone novices are assembled deep in the forest miles away from the Shoshone camp. The season of Ninja training is to commence. Yuji sits mounted on a Mustang and eyes the young men - all eager and ready. He waves his hand for them to follow and then charges through the forest with the young braves in hard pursuit. Yuji keeps the horse at a pace the braves can manage as they run over the forest trails, rugged terrain and shallow river beds. Yuji looks back to keep an eye on the trainees, the young men are challenged and tested as they try to keep up with Yuji on horseback. Yuji rides out of the trees and across the rolling grassland, the young braves are sweaty and strained, and follow a distance back. Yuji enters camp and rides to the Chief's central tepee where Buffalo Sky and the Elders are standing, he dismounts and joins them in waiting. Soon, they see a weary and worn bunch of braves slowly run toward them, many barely able to move their legs, all are winded, huffing and puffing. Finally, the braves reach Yuji and the tribe leaders - and collapse on the ground gasping for air. Yuji glances over at Buffalo Sky, the Elders, Bear Claw, Jumping Horse and the others. Yuji grins and remarks, "Good! No one abandoned. Everyone finished the run (he smiles) Now, that I know what I have. We can begin the Ninja training!" Jumping Horse translates Yuji's remarks to the leaders. Buffalo Sky and the leaders watch as the young men regain their strength and stand to their feet - alert, awaiting Yuji's instructions. the Chief and the leaders look at Yuji and nod their approval.

Over the succeeding weeks, months and years, Yuji puts the Shoshone braves through gruelling training to test their metal and to instil strength, agility and skill. Yuji has the braves lash together long branches and instructs them to stand, balance and walk along them. Many fall off. He makes them stand for hours at a time exposed to the hot sun, the driving rain and the cold of night. Some collapse to the ground, their leg muscles no longer hold them up. In a dry riverbed, Yuji instructs them to grip and carry big heavy stones to build strong arms. The Ninja Master teaches the recruits to run, jump, flip, twirl and summersault. Soon, the braves become quick and agile! Yuji instructs the braves in hand-to-hand combat. The volunteers who attack get their lumps - The other trainees playfully tease each other. Over time, the braves become skilled at combat and learn to grapple and toss their opponent, throw punches, deliver kicks, block and deflect attacks, and apply chokeholds. Sometimes, a brave gets floored during training and the others laugh and poke fun. As the seasons change, Yuji teaches the braves to make and use camouflage as Ninja strategy, white outfits for the Winter, brown clothing for the Fall, green apparel for the Spring, and black outfits for concealment night and day. As the trainees get older, stronger, tougher, Yuji makes them run through knee-high snow, swim swift flowing rivers, and run hard and long in the hot sun. On many occasions, at a grassy elevation near a waterfall, Yuji and the Shoshone trainees sit in a circle - deep in peaceful meditation. With the recruits toughened and hardened through the rigorous training - Yuji now introduces weapons. He shows them the skills and techniques to use the staff, knife, tomahawk, spear, war club, bow and arrow - and lastly, the Ninja swords. The braves begin training by using wood swords. Yuji instructs on proper stance, foot placement and balance. He teaches them to use the sword for offence and defence during battle situations. Yuji observes closely as the braves wield their wood swords to block, deflect and disarm their opponent. He watches intently as the braves swing their swords to attack, overpower and defeat their enemy. The Ninja Master is very pleased with their progress.

For the final and most important phase on training, Yuji introduces the trainees to the steel swords used for battle - the short Ninjato sword and the long Katana sword. He passes the Ninjato and Katana swords around so each trainee can see and feel each sword in his hand. Yuji carefully demonstrates the Ninja techniques and tactical skill for both swords. The recruits keenly watch as Yuji holds each sword to spin, twirl, slice and chop the blade at an imaginary enemy. One day as the recruits gather at their training ground, Yuji motions for them to follow. He leads them into the forest some distance until they arrive at a large clearing. In the centre of the vacant ground Yuji has created a homemade forge complete with bellows, tongs, anvil, hammer and a large basin of water. A few yards from the forge sits large sacks, one with iron sand and the other with chunks of coal. Near the sacks are three blocks of wood, each contains a different waterstone used to grind and polish the steel blade. Yuji steps into the middle beside the forge and he motions the trainees to fan out and sit down. As the braves sit down on the ground, Yuji lights the coals of the forge to start a fire, then he puts portions of iron sand and coal together in a metal cauldron and sets it in the flames. All the trainees carefully watch as Yuji carries out the forging operation, working the bellows to increase the heat to melt the mixture into molten metal. When ready, Yuji grabs the tongs and moves the cauldron of red hot liquid metal over to a mould set in the earth, then he pours out the molten steel into the blade-shaped cavity. Yuji repeats this process until molten metal rises to the top of the blade shaped form. The heat of the forge and the hard work makes Yuji perspire. He wipes sweat from his brow and continues. He checks the mould to inspect if the metal is ready. With tongs, he extracts the crude red hot steel from the mould and brings it to the anvil. He picks up the hammer and hits the hot metal repeatedly, hammering, striking, bending and shaping the glowing metal bar into the recognizable shape of a Katana sword. Each trainee is mesmerized to witness the sword making process. Yuji hammers the steel, returns the blade to the hot coals, removes it again and hammers it more. At times Yuji dunks the hot steel into the basin of water and steam gushes out, then he brings out the smouldering metal. After Yuji has hammered and bent the steel into the shape of a Katana sword, he stops and looks at his trainees - then he holds up the katana blade for all to see. The recruits shout cries of victory and celebration as Yuji displays the newly created sword. Over the week, Yuji and the trainees gather at the forge and the braves watch as Yuji uses the waterstones to grind and further prepare the blade. He slides and presses the blade against the waterstones to remove layers of metal to produce the edge needed for a Japanese Katana sword. Yuji closely inspects the improved finish of the steel blade, when he started out it was rough cold black metal, but after skillful use of the waterstones, Yuji now holds a gleaming highly polished Katana steel blade. He presents it for the Ninja trainees to examine - everyone is in awe.

Finally, the day arrives for the Shoshone Ninja trainees to face their ultimate test - trial by combat! The Chief and the Elders have agreed that Yuji will choose one trainee to fight and defeat five Shoshone braves. Once again, excited villagers gather to watch a special event - how a Shoshone Ninja trainee will perform in actual combat with proven warriors. There is so much anticipation in the air, it's almost palatable. The people stand in a large circle with the fighters in the middle of a wide open area. The Ninja Master walks to the group of trainees, all are poised and ready. Yuji looks into their eyes as he scans each one, with his decision made, Yuji picks Otter to do battle. At one side, Bear Claw stands with five braves selected for their prowess and fighting ability. Yuji sends in Otter. As Otter stands and faces the five braves, Yuji looks at Jumping Horse and nods. Jumping Horse cries out, "Let the contest begin!" The five braves move toward Otter and spread out. Otter takes a fighting stance and waits. As one brave runs at him with a knife, Otter sidesteps and trips the attacker sending him into the dirt. The brave jumps to his feet and violently swipes the knife blade. Otter dodges and strikes the assailant with a flurry of blows to knock him out. Then, two braves lunge in at the same time, Otter quickly spins to kick one unconscious and strikes the other with disabling blows. Otter looks at the two remaining braves, one rushes at him with a tomahawk and swings it back and forth. Otter blocks the tomahawk and wrenches the braves arm, then leans backward to catapult the attacker to hit the ground hard yards away. Otter turns toward the last attacker, a big brave with a spear. The huge brave swipes the spear tip at Otter's face to force him further and further back. Otter watches his opponent carefully. As the brave repeatedly thrusts the sharp spear, Otter quickly ducks and moves with powerful strikes to greatly stun the big brave. As the brute teeters back and forth, Otter steps up and takes the spear from his opponent's hand as the brave falls over into the dirt. Thud! Otter stands alone as the contest champion! All the people break out with Shoshone cries of victory, celebration and honour. Yuji approaches Buffalo Sky, the Elders, Bear Claw, Thunder Cloud, Two Knives, and the other leaders - they beam with pride. Yuji comes up to the Chief and leaders, bows low and lifts up with a big smile. Buffalo Sky calls Jumping Horse to tell Yuji, "Our braves can fight like you - like Ninja!" As Jumping Horse translates, Yuji remarks to Buffalo Sky, "This is **KAISHI - The Beginning!** Now, these new warriors can teach others." When the Chief hears Yuji's reply, he carefully attempts the pronunciation, "Kai-shi". Yuji responds, "Aho! Yes! Kaishi." Buffalo Sky smiles and remarks, "This is good! Our people can remain strong and well protected!" Yuji bows, leaves the Tribe leaders and walks over to Otter and the other trainees to congratulate and dismisses them. Each young brave is jubilant and relieved that they have passed the Final Test!

CHAPTER TWENTY-FOUR
Shoshone Ninja Graduation

The Graduation Day has arrived!

The trainees are arranged in a straight line, each kneels on a woven mat. Each dressed in a black Ninja outfit with their own Ninja sword at the side. The entire village surrounds them in silence - respectful of this solemn and special occasion. Chief Buffalo Sky, the Elders and the lead warriors observe with a deep sense of pride and satisfaction. In the open area, Yuji kneels dressed in a ceremonial kimono with a glossy lacquered red Katana sword in a wood cradle before him. Bouquets of flowers decorate the perimeter of his large mat. Yuji begins to chant and sing Japanese words as he lights incense sticks and makes five circular motions, and then bows. The Ninja Master returns upright and fastens his gaze on the row of black clad graduates before him. Yuji loudly speaks the Japanese word for trainees, "Kenshusei!" All the trainees bow and reply in unison with the Japanese word for Teacher, "Sensei!" The graduates raise themselves up. Yuji runs his eyes along the line of Shoshone young men, then he cries out the Japanese word for warrior, "Bushi." All the trainees bow a second time and together reply, "Hai!" Next, Yuji reaches out and lifts the red Katana sword from the cradle and holds it out with both arms. Each trainee grabs his sword and holds it out in front like the Sensei. Yuji loudly cries - "Ninja!" All the trainees reply in unison with the Japanese word for I pledge, "Chigiri!" Yuji makes a second declaration, "Ninja! - Ninja!" The young men reply loudly as a united group, "Chigiri! - Chigiri! Yuji holds the red Katana in both hands and bows low and remains. All the graduates with swords in both hands bow low and remain. After a moment of silence, save only the sound of the wind and forest birds chirping, Yuji raises up and rings a bronze bell to signal the young men can return upright. Yuji looks out at the graduates with a big smile, each one returns his gaze with deep respect. Yuji bows one last time and the graduates bow in return, then Yuji looks over at Jumping Horse and nods. Jumping Horse steps out from the ranks, points to the row of young men and lifts up his voice, "Today, we celebrate - we eat, sing and dance - our tribe now have Shoshone Ninja warriors!" All the camp erupts with loud cries of victory, joy and jubilation! The people and family members move out to congratulate their new warriors. This is a very special day in the history of the tribe.

CHAPTER TWENTY-FIVE
Buffalo Hunt

The villagers are busy with morning routines when Two Knives and another brave ride into Camp from the eastern grasslands. The two men ride their mounts past the tepees and head directly to the Chief's dwelling; they quickly dismount and go inside. The commotion peeks the interest and curiosity of many and soon a number of people congregate near the Chief's tepee. Within a few moments; Buffalo Sky, the Elders, Two Knives and Bear Claw emerge to face the growing crowd of men, women and warriors. Hushed comments and chatter ripple through the crowd. The Chief holds high his arm and the people become quiet. Buffalo Sky raises his voice for all to hear, "Our scouts have found the Buffalo herd - three days ride from camp." The villagers become stirred at the news. Shoshone warriors yell out hunting cries with excitement! Bear Claw exclaims, "We will kill many Buffalo. This winter, our tepees will have meat and fur." Braves from across the village gather on horseback and raise their rifles, bows and spears in the air with cheers. A warrior brings over the Chief's horse and Buffalo Sky mounts up and looks around at his people, "The Shoshone ride to hunt Buffalo!" The warriors on horses are eager and ready with their weapons. The Chief glances at his mounted braves, then he waves his arm and they all charge forward and ride out of camp. The men, women and children watch as the Hunting Party head toward the eastern grasslands.

The Shoshone braves ride across an ocean of rolling grassland stretching out as far as the eye can see. On the horizon, Buffalo Sky and the warriors see a lone figure riding toward them, soon the silhouette of horse and rider becomes more clear, everyone can recognize it is Two Knives. The veteran scout rides up to the Chief and Bear Claw, he's breathing rapidly and his eyes are energized, "The Buffalo herd is large. They graze not far away." Bear Claw turns to everyone, "We will approach quietly not to stampede the herd." Two Knives points in the direction and the Shoshone ride off. They follow Two Knives as he leads them down into a deep grassy gully where they keep moving until he lifts his arm to stop. Two Knives points to the hilltop. All the Shoshone dismount and quietly lead and walk their horses to just below the grassy ridge. As a brave holds their horse reins, Buffalo Sky and Bear Claw crawl up to peer over the crest of the gully. Before their eyes are thousands of Buffalo - enormous Bull Buffalos, female Buffalos and their small calves. The large herd graze upon the lush grass and move at a slow pace. The Chief and Bear Claw return to their horses and stand ready. The Shoshone braves grab their horse reins and await the Chief's signal. Buffalo Sky looks at Two Knives who nods. The Chief waves his arm and all the Shoshone quickly mount up and sprint their horses over the crest of the hill and descend upon the slowly moving herd in a surprise attack! The Buffalo herd becomes alarmed and swiftly run from the oncoming danger. Shoshone warriors bravely ride beside and between the huge beasts as the animals criss-cross and jostle about. The herd thunders forward making the very ground shake and tremble. Braves ride among the animals and kill the Buffalo firing their rifles, shooting their arrows and thrusting their spears. Riding among the stampeding herd is extremely dangerous and a Shoshone brave collides with a large Bison. The brave is thrown from his horse and trampled to death. The Shoshone chase the herd until Bear Claw signals enough. The Chief and braves stop and regroup. They look across the grassland and see the many fallen Buffalo - the Shoshone braves yell loud victory cries into the air. Buffalo Sky turns his gaze to his warriors, "We took many Buffalo today, but the herd took our Shoshone brother. We will remember him in our hunting songs." The braves acknowledge with head nods. Then the Chief motions and all the braves break into groups of twos and threes. They ride to their kill and begin to skin and butcher the slain Buffalo. Bear Claw looks at the Chief, "This winter, our people will be warm and have plenty of food." The Chief gently smiles as he watches the braves collect their hunt trophies, "It has always been this way! The Shoshone and the Buffalo are joined together in life." The sounds of the rejoicing hunters carry far across the plains. The Shoshone make travos and secure the poles to the horses. They pack on the butchered meat and buffalo furs to create heavy loads. The Hunting Party will travel back home at a much slower pace, the riders on horses fitted travos must ride with extra care. Buffalo Sky and the warriors beam with great happiness as they journey back to their village.

CHAPTER TWENTY-SIX
The Chetowa Of The North

Far up in the distant north, in the lands that belong to the Tribe known as the Chetowa, a raiding party on horseback are gathered outside the tepee of Chief Kicking Horse. The Chief and his son, Spotted Bird, a strong young brave, emerge from the dwelling. The son looks at his father, "We travel to new territory - past the land of the Crow." The Chief smiles, "Good hunting my son! Bring back many horses." Spotted Bird grabs the reins and jumps onto his horse and gazes down at his father, "Catches Snake and Running Dog go with us. They know the lands and say there are many horses." Spotted Bird turns about to the warriors and waves his arm. As the raiding party race off with whoops and cries of excitement, Kicking Horse and the Chetowa Elders watch as they leave camp.

On the second day, the Chetowa enter central Wyoming and the land of the Crow. The Chetowa raiding party travel across the grassy plains until they meet a small band of Crow braves. The two groups stop a distance from each other and wait. According to an ancient custom, when braves from another Indian tribe meet, there is be an exchange of gifts to signify good will and peaceful intentions. Catches Snake glances over at Spotted Dog, then moves his horse forward at a slow careful pace. At the same time, the Crow brave moves his horse forward. The Chetowa warrior and the Crow warrior slowly ride to a few yards of one another and stop. Catches Snake holds up a tomahawk and watches as the Crow brave lifts up a tobacco pipe. With the items still held high, the two warriors steer their horses until their mounts are beside each other. Catches Snake offers the tomahawk handle first and the Crow warrior extends the tobacco pipe. They both exchange items and part, each returning to their group. When Catches

Snake reaches Spotted Dog and the Chetowa, they watch as the Crow braves let out whoops and cries as they ride off in the opposite direction. Catches Snake smiles, "Soon, we will enter the far lands. Fine horse are there." Spotted Dog nods, "We will take many. Our people will sing songs about us and speak our names with pride." Spotted Dog looks about and motions forward and the Chetowa resume their trek across the plains.

Two Days pass.

The Chetowa raiding party hide in the grass as Running Dog, Catches Snake and Spotted Bird spy out the camp before them. The men see only a few braves and some old men. As they study the Indian village, Spotted Bird become wide-eyed as he sees Bright Star walk from her tepee to fetch water at the river. Spotted Bird turns his head and looks at the Chetowa braves, "The maiden with silver in her hair is mine! You can pick from the others." The raiding party acknowledge the young leader's claim. Catches Snake comments, "Running Dog and I will get the horses." Spotted Bird quickly remarks, "The other braves and I will capture the maidens." The Chetowa divide into two groups, Catches Snake leads one group off while Spotted Dog and the others descend on the unsuspecting camp. In the village, the people are about their daily routines, when suddenly - they hear loud whoops, yells and war cries. The villagers look to see strange warriors bearing down on them. The women and children flee to their dwellings. Bright Star races back to her tepee. The young braves and the few old men brace to defend their village. The fighting and tussling does not last long. In the short skirmish, a zealous young brave and a stubborn old man are killed, the rest are overpowered and unharmed. Spotted Bird rides up and dismounts outside Eagle Feather's tepee. The young brave boldly enters and is confronted by Bright Star holding a knife and standing as far away as possible. Spotted Bird suddenly stops - struck by her beauty. As he strides over, she raises the knife, screams and attacks. Spotted Bird easily overpowers her and takes the knife away. He picks her up and puts her over his shoulder and exits. Outside the tepee, Spotted Bird holds Bright Star as he ties her hands. He lays her across the pony and then binds her feet with rawhide cords. Spotted Bird jumps on his horse and looks around. The other Chetowa also have captured maidens. Catches Snake and Running Dog and their group ride up with many horses in tow. The Chief's son declares, "We found good hunting! Many will sing our names around the camp fires." The raiding party let loose loud victory cries and ride off with the maidens and horses.

CHAPTER TWENTY-SEVEN
Shoshone Warriors Pursue

The next day…

Chief Buffalo Sky and the Shoshone hunting party ride over the grassy crest and come into camp with their horses pulling travos piled high with meat and Buffalo furs. The Chief and the warriors are puzzled that the villagers are not greeting them with shouts of joy; instead, the people have sad expressions indicating something is wrong. As the Chief draws close to the middle of camp near the large tepee, Elders approach him with downcast faces. Buffalo Sky asks, "Why are your hearts so heavy at our return? We have much meat and furs!" An Elder steps out and looks directly at the Chief, "When you and our braves were hunting Buffalo, a raiding party stole our maidens and horses." Buffalo Sky and the warrior's expressions turn to anger and rage. Buffalo Sky cries out, "What maidens were taken?" The Elder cast his eyes down to the ground, he can barely get the words out, "They took Foxtail's oldest daughter, Singing Rain, Two Knives' sister Willow, and many others." The Elder looks at Eagle Feather, "Bright Star was also taken!" Eagle Feather, Yuji and Bear Claw are stunned by the news and rush their mounts up beside the Chief's horse. Bear Claw strongly urges, "We must send warriors after them now, before they get too far!" Buffalo Sky looks out at the gathered villagers, the women weep for their daughters, and the fathers and old people look at him with despair. Yuji speaks up, "Let me and the Shoshone Ninja help rescue the maidens." Eagle Feather adds, "I know Yuji cares greatly for Bright Star. Let him ride with me." The Chief turns to Bear Claw, "Take our warriors, Yuji and The Shoshone Ninja, and go after them. I will remain with our people for their hearts are broken." A rescue party is quickly formed as warriors run to tepees to gather weapons, clothing and provisions of food. Yuji races to his tepee, enters and grabs the Ninjato and Katana swords, bow, quiver of arrows, and some leather pouches. He exits and runs back and mounts his horse, ready to ride. Bear Claw, Eagle Feather, Thunder Cloud, Two Knives, Yuji and the Shoshone warriors assemble on horses near the Chief's tepee. Buffalo Sky emerges and lifts his arm high, "Ride swift. Be strong. Fight well. Return our daughters to us!" The Shoshone let loose loud yelps, whoops and war cries as they ride with haste and steely resolve.

Somewhere across the vast plains and rolling hills, the Chetowa warriors ride steady, their horses show fatigue. Running Dog and Catches Snake ride up beside Spotted Bird. Running Dog relays his worry, "Our horses are tired. They need water and rest." The young Chetowa leader looks at Catches Snake for his advice, "What he says his true. Our horses will need all their strength to reach our lands." Spotted Bird glances over his shoulder at the weary group, "Find water and rest the horses. Have braves see we are not being followed." Running Dog reins his horse around and sends out a scout to help find water. Next, he dispatches four braves as a rearguard. As the Chetowa continue riding, Bright Star nonchalantly looks about, with no one watching, she chews a piece of rawhide off her binding and spits it out. No one notices the piece of leather fall to the ground. The scout that Running Dog sent out, rides over a hill and sees a small stream at the bottom of the gully. The scout races back and rides up to Spotted Bird and points, "Fresh water not far!" Spotted Bird waves his hand and the Chetowa head in that direction. They reach the gully and dismount to water their horses, themselves - and then their captives.

Following in hot pursuit, the Shoshone ride hard to catch the perpetrators, their horses are tired and sweaty. They stop near some large rocks. Two Knives dismounts and walks the terrain looking for clues, he checks the tracks and notices the deep hoof impressions in the dirt. He looks at Bear Claw and the others, "They went this way. Some tracks show horses carry two people." Bear Claw reins his horse around to look at the group, "Soon, we will catch those who stole our women and horses. He glances over at Eagle Feather and Yuji, "We will bring back Bright Star and the other maidens!" The Shoshone braves launch out with renewed determination and let out yells, whoops and war cries!

* * *

The landscape changes from grasslands and rolling hills to that of higher elevation with rugged terrain. Spotted Bird and the Chetowa are now leaving Crow territory. The north highlands lay ahead in the distance. The high country forces the horses to follow closer together and move slower over the rough ground; this allows Bright Star to make eye contact with the other maidens. She shows courage to help and assure the others. As the ponies get beside each other, Bright Star gets Willow's attention and whispers, "Our warriors are not far behind. They will rescue us. Soon, we will be free." Willow and Singing Rain both nod and manage a faint smile. The Chetowa keep winding their way up the escarpment when Catches Snake rides up to the column front, "I found a good place to make camp." Spotted Bird turns to glance back at the group, "Good! We can rest and travel at sunrise." Catches Snake then leads them to the site he selected. At the spot, the Chetowa tie their horses and Running Dog makes a small fire, the surrounding rocks hide it from view. The braves set the maidens on the ground in a group and post guards to watch them. With horses and maidens secure, the Chetowa warriors relax and rest around the fire's glowing embers.

The day draws to a close and light grows dim. Bear Claw and the Shoshone try to follow the tracks but it's dusk and daylight is fleeting. Seeing is difficult and Two Knives remarks, "It is too dark for tracking." Bear Claw relies, "We will camp here, rest our horses and start fresh in the morning." The Shoshone braves dismount, tie the horses and make a camp fire. Some of the braves stand guard while the other warriors take their rest. Yuji walks up onto a rock ledge and looks out into the night, into the direction they pursue. Eagle Feather approaches, "Two Knives is our best tracker! They will not escape us. We will get Bright Star and the others." Yuji looks at the older man, "We do not know these Indians. I worry that she might be harmed." Eagle Feather positions himself beside Yuji and the two men stare out into the dark night.

The rays of the morning sun streak across the sky as the Chetowa break camp and get their horses and captives ready. Running Dog and Catches Snakes ride up and the young man remarks. "Soon, we will reach our village. Kicking Horse will be pleased at our success!" The warriors whoop in response. The raiding party promptly launch out toward their lands.

* * *

At first light, the Shoshone braves make ready their horses and weapons. Bear Claw motions to the group, "We must ride fast to catch them!" The warriors acknowledge and release strong war cries and bolt their steads forward to give chase. As the Shoshone ride over a knoll, Two Knives is off his horse and inspects the ground. He picks something up and holds it high for the others to see. Bear Claw, Eagle Feather and Yuji ride up, "Look! I've found chewed rawhide. Someone left this." He passes it to Bear Claw and he examines the small teeth marks and replies, "One of the maidens left us a sign to follow. - Hurry!" The Shoshone rally and race ahead in the direction where Two Knives points.

CHAPTER TWENTY-EIGHT
The Chetowa Camp

Spotted Bird and the Chetowa begin to see familiar terrain and landmarks as their horses get more north. Spotted Bird glances down at Bright Star slung across his horse, "Soon, you will be my squaw, cook my meals, and bear many young braves." Bright Star clenches her teeth with defiance, "I will never be your woman! My heart belongs to another." The young leader turns and looks behind, then he returns his gaze, "We will be deep in Chetowa lands. No one is behind us. Your people are far away." With his pronouncement made, Spotted Bird nudges his horse and quickens the pace. The raiding party travel down the escarpment, along a river, through a forest, and onto a large savannah - then the raiding party stop. Before them lay the sprawling Chetowa village with a great many tepees. Scores of people mill about. Chetowa villagers at the edge of camp cry out, "Spotted Bird and the warriors return!" One man tells his young son, "Run. Tell Kicking Horse and the others that our braves have returned." The lad races through the tepees and disappears. As the raiding party steer their horses through camp, villagers come out of dwellings to welcome them back. The people see the bound maidens and the many horses in tow. Spotted Bird, Catches Snake and Running Dog smile proudly. Excitement floods the camp! Soon a swarm of people follow, young people and children playfully accompany the returning warriors. Ahead at the large central tepee, Kicking Horse and the Chetowa Elders emerge from the structure and watch the procession approach. Spotted Bird and the braves stop yards away. The Chief sees the maidens and horses, "Welcome my son! We are happy to see your hunt was a success!" Spotted Bird manoeuvres his horse to display Bright Star, "I claim this one for myself. She will become my squaw!" Bright Star become feisty at his words and struggles to get free. Kicking

Horse, the Elders and the people break out laughing. The Chief remarks in a teasing manner, "This one is a wildcat! You will have much work to do." Spotted Bird grins and slaps Bright Star's behind, "She will soon learn her place." Bright Star gets fuming mad. The Elders and Kicking Horse continue to chuckle as the braves take the maidens into the tepee next door. Some of the maidens resist with shrieks and screams, but to no avail.

Inside the tepee, Spotted Bird and the braves set the maidens down and tie them together as a group. Willow, Singing Rain and Bright Star show defiance, while some of the girls cry tears. As the warriors exit the tepee, Spotted Bird looks at Catches Snake, "Have two braves outside guarding at all times." Catches Snake nods and selects two braves as guards. The others in the raiding party go off to their own tepees. Spotted Bird walks over to his Father's dwelling and steps inside. Kicking Horse and the Elders are talking when Spotted Bird enters, the Chief looks at his son, "The maidens will make good squaws for our braves." The Elders nod agreement. The young man steps closer, "I will marry the one who fights. She will bear me strong children." Kicking Horse motions his hand, "Sit with us and tell of your journey." Spotted Bird lowers himself to take a place in the circle.

CHAPTER TWENTY-NINE

The Shoshone Rescue

The Shoshone carefully travel through the strange new territory, Two Knives informs the group they are in the land of the Chetowa. He reads the trail signs and leads them to the Chetowa village. The vast camp stretches out before them, it's much larger than their Shoshone camp back home. Bear Claw, Thunder Cloud, Eagle Feather and Yuji hide and spy to gather information. From the high elevation, they see the braves that guard the dwelling beside the large central tepee. The Shoshone rescuers decide to wait until just before sunrise to free the maidens. During the early twilight hours, the Shoshone get ready to enact their plan while it's still dark. Bear Claw looks at the others, "Thunder Cloud and I will scatter their horses." Yuji replies, "Eagle Feather, the Ninja warriors and I, will free Bright Star and the others." Bear Claw nods and the Shoshone split into two groups and strike out. Bear Claw's group sneak up near the big horse coral, and Two Knives and Thunder Cloud knock out the sentries. The Shoshone braves remove the thorn barricades to create a wide opening. Bear Claw and his group enter the horse compound to scare and stampede the horses by waving hands and bows. The large horse herd spook and race off toward camp. Bear Claw turns to the group, "We must rejoin with Eagle Feather and the others." Meanwhile, Yuji, Eagle Feather and the Shoshone Ninja sneak through the camp, quietly moving past tepee after tepee. They avoid detection and silence any encountered Chetowa. Their group reach within a few feet of the maiden's tepee. Suddenly, loud cries and yells fill the air, "Horses are loose! The horses are getting away. Everybody help!" There's mayhem and confusion as the horses stampede through the Chetowa camp. People exit tepees and try to stop the runaway horses. When the sentries at the maiden's tepee get distracted, Yuji and a Ninja warrior knock out the guards.

Bright Star and the maidens hear the commotion outside and become frightened. Suddenly, the entry flap lifts and Yuji appears. Bright Star breaks into an overjoyed smile. The other girls are happy and relieved as Yuji, Eagle Feather and a Shoshone brave untie them. The Shoshone Ninjas stand guard outside. Eagle Feather looks at the maidens, "We must hurry! Bear Claw has troubled their horses so we can escape." The group quickly exit the tepee. The entire camp is in turmoil and chaos. Chetowa braves attempt to capture their valuable loose horses. In the confusion, the rescue party sneak through the tepees in the dark. Coming around some dwellings at the edge of camp, they run into a group of Chetowa warriors who attack! Yuji and the Shoshone Ninja swiftly defeat the Chetowa with their Martial Arts skills. With the woods nearby, the Shoshone escape into the forest and rendezvous with Bear Claw, Thunder Cloud, Two Knives and the others. Together and reunited, the Shoshone steal away.

The Chetowa braves are busy everywhere cornering and collecting their all important mounts. Spotted Bird bolts into the tepee and sees it empty, the maidens are gone - he exits in a screaming rage! Kicking Horse and Chetowa warriors quickly rally around, "I will not loose my prized woman! We must ride out now." The Chief turns to Catches Snake, "Assemble our warriors. We will hunt them down and reclaim the maidens." Chetowa warriors run to tepees to collect weapons and provisions and then rally back, mounted and ready to ride. Running Dog and others yell loud yelps and war cries! The shroud of twilight gives way to the light of the early morning sun. Kicking Horse climbs up and spins his horse around and lifts the War Lance high in the air. The Chetowa war party ride off with a vengeance!

The Shoshone rescuers race through Chetowa lands, speeding through forests, crossing rivers and climbing high plains. Bear Claw and Two Knives use their wilderness skills and tricks to cover their horse tracks. Next, Two Knives and some others create a false trail to misdirect the pursuers. As the rescue party press on, they go over rolling hills, plains, rivers and flat-top buttes. Yuji and Bright Star ride beside each other. The pretty maiden speaks softly, "My heart was glad to see you!" Yuji's eyes his sweetheart, "Your freedom and safety mean everything to me." Bright Star reaches out to touch Yuji's arm.

Behind them.

Catches Snake and Running Dog examine the ground for clues. Running Dog finds a mountain shrub with a broken branch. He stands and points in that direction. Kicking Horse, Spotted Bird and the Chetowa resume their chase. The Chetowa ford streams, ride down ravines and across grassy plains. Their pursuit stops at a stream - the trail cold. Catches Snake slowly rides his horse into the middle of the shallow stream and studies the riverbed - he suddenly stops. Mossy rocks are overturned. He looks over to Kicking Horse and points down the stream, "They went this way! Their horses turned over the rocks." Kicking Horse waves his arm and the War Party ride their horses into the water and follow the stream.

Up ahead.

The Shoshone gallop over hills and through ravines until they find a pond to water their horses and quench their thirst. Bear Claw climbs up onto the rocks to view the land ahead. The elevation descends toward the lower grasslands and wide open plains. He comments to those nearby, "We will cross the land of the Crow. They may stop us." When the horses have drank their fill and everyone has been refreshed, the Shoshone mount up and ride out. Travelling the lower grasslands, Two Knives brings his mount alongside Yuji and Eagle Feather, "That was the last water hole until we reach our border." Eagle Feather remarks, "We must not push our horses past their strength. Without water the horses will die." Yuji looks at Eagle Feather, "If what Two Knives said is true - the Chetowa will also water their horses there." Eagle Feather nods, "Yes! The other water holes are in Crow lands. Why do you speak this?" Yuji chimes, "Eagle Feather, follow me." Yuji and Eagle Feather gallop up to Bear Claw at the front of the group. Bear Claw sees Yuji's expression, "Is something wrong Yuji?" The Ninja Master replies, "I have an idea to slow down those who chase us!" Bear Claw asks, "What is it?" Yuji replies, "Let me and Eagle Feather return to the last water hole. There is something I must do." The Leader scans around at the group, "We will move at a steady pace not to strain the horses. When you finish - quickly join us." Yuji nods, and he and Eagle Feather ride off in the direction they came from, going past the group. As Yuji rides past Bright Star, they exchange glances. Eagle Feather and Yuji ride hard and retrace their trail back to the watering hole. Approaching close to the water hole, they quietly make their way to the site. They scan about and see no one is there - it's safe!

Yuji swiftly dismounts and goes to the edge of the pond. He reaches into the pouch on his side and brings out a handful of black powder and scatters it across the water. The black dust sits momentarily on the surface then dissolves into the water. He turns and looks at Eagle Feather who is dismounted with his ear to the ground, "Riders are not far away. We must leave now!" Yuji and Eagle Feather jump on their horse and gallop off in haste.

In a distance behind, Spotted Bird and Kicking Horse lead the Chetowa onward. Up ahead, Catches Snake and Running Dog search for tracks. Catches Snake waves his arm to follow. Before long, the Chetowa War Party ride over the ridge and down to the pool of water. The horses are sweaty and tired, the braves are weary and worn out from the chase. The pond is not large enough for all the horses and warriors. While the first group gather around the pond, Kicking Horse, Spotted Bird and the others wait. As the horses and warriors drink long and hard to quench their thirst - suddenly, the front legs of one horse buckle - another horse lets out a loud neigh and keels over to fall on a brave. Within seconds, other horses collapse to their knees. A number of braves begin to crumple over grabbing their stomach and groaning - a few vomit! Kicking Horse runs to the pond and waves his arms, "Stop! Don't drink! The water's bad." Spotted Bird and Catches Snake examine the fallen horses and ill warriors. Catches Snake shakes his head, "These cannot ride! We must find other water before going on." Spotted Bird become frustrated and agitated, "The Shoshone are ahead - we can catch them!" Running Dog comes beside the young leader, "Without water - our horses and warriors will have no strength to fight. We must find water." Spotted Bird reluctantly agrees and mounts his horse. The Chief looks at the warriors, "Catches Snake and Running Dog will find us water. We will follow them." Kicking Horses orders the braves and horses that became ill to stay behind at the pond. Catches Snake and Running Dog start to head north, opposite the direction of the chase, the Chetowa war party wearily plod behind. After a number of hours, Catches Snake and Running Dog find a small waterfall. The Chetowa quench their parched throats and liberally water the horses. The warriors are bone tired and rest a good while. Watching the group lay about idle and still, Spotted Bird grows impatient and strides into their midst and looks about, "We must hurry to catch them!" The young man looks over at his father, "They are getting away!" Kicking Horse sees the anguish in Spotted Bird's face, the Chief grabs his horse's mane and mounts up, "Get on your horses - we ride!" The Chetowa warriors quickly rise and get on their horses and race off with Kicking Horse and Spotted Bird leading them.

CHAPTER THIRTY
The Rescue Party In Crow Lands

Bear Claw and the Shoshone cross the Great Plain grasslands - an expanse of rolling hills and vales. They are in the bottom of a vale and ride slow and steady when a group of Crow braves ride over the hill crest. The Crows stop on the grassy ridge and study the travelling Shoshone. Bear Claw spots the Crow party and turns to the others, "Stay clam and do not act hostile. They must see we only want to pass through." The Crow braves yell whoops and yelps as they ride down the slope and gallop circles around the slow moving group. The Shoshone stop and remain calm as Bear Claw instructed. The Crow regroup and approach - they halt their horses a hundred yards away. Both Indian groups study each other. Then the Crow leader rides forward and stops thirty feet away. Bear Claw raises his arm high with an open palm - and slowly rides out and stops ten feet from the Crow brave. The two warriors look at one another. Bear Claw lifts up his beaded buckskin pouch over his head and offers it to the Crow brave. The Crow warrior scrutinizes Bear Claw, then the Crow brave offers his bone handle hunting knife. Bear Claw gently nods and slowly moves his horse forward, and the Crow brave slowly moves his horse ahead. As the two reach side by side, Bear Claw extends the beaded pouch and the Crow warrior offers the bone knife at the same time. Both men exchange their traded items. The Crow brave sprints off to rejoin his friends, and they ride up over the ridge and disappear. Bear Claw returns to the Shoshone group, "It is safe now. They will not bother us." The Shoshone warriors and maidens resume their trek home.

CHAPTER THIRTY-ONE
Guns and Gold

Cutter and his gang rob an overland stage coach. The outlaws point their pistols and rifles at the driver, shotgun and five passengers; the Eastern travellers are scared out of their wits. One outlaw climbs onto the stage coach and shoves the big strongbox off the roof. Thud! He jumps down and shoots off the lock and pries open the lid and looks inside - Empty! Cutter walks over and stares at the empty hollow interior and becomes angry. He points his gun at the driver's head and pulls back the hammer, "Where's the gold, ole' timer?" The man gripped with fear can barely get the words out, "The Mine sent it by train! The owners decided last minute." One bandit can hardly believe it, "What - No Gold?!" The badmen become livid and starts to murmur and complain. Cutter turns to his gang, "Well boys, you know what to do!" Cutter pivots and shoots the driver square in the forehead. The outlaws begin to empty their guns and rifles killing all. The bodies of the shotgun, three women and two male passengers are riddled with bullets. Cutter and the gang look at the bloody mess with cold callous eyes. Cutter motions his arm and the outlaws ride off.

CHAPTER THIRTY-TWO

Shoshone Take The Long Way

The Shoshone wake up from a good night's sleep. Bear Claw and Two knives are bent down over a patch of earth as Two Knives draws in the sand, "This is the route ahead. We pass too close to the Crow village. Dangerous!" Thunder Cloud looks at the sand markings, "Is there another route away from the Crow?" Two Knives glances up at his friend and draws another line in the sand, "There is another way, but it will take longer." Bear Claw studies the two drawings with a pensive look - then stands up, "Better to avoid the Crow and take the longer route!" Two Knives adds, "The longer way will be safer for our maidens." They all agree and go to mount their horses. Atop his stead, Bear Claw looks at everyone, "We take the longer route to go around the Crow. We cannot risk any trouble in their lands." The Shoshone braves and maidens get on their horses and they head out as Bear Claw and Two Knives lead the way.

Across the plains, Kicking Horse and the Chetowa race to cover ground to make up for lost time. Ahead in the distance, Catches Snake and Running Dog find Shoshone tracks. The large Chetowa war party quicken their pursuit across the grassy plains and over wilderness streams. The Chetowa group see Catches Snake and Running Dog stop. Upon approach, Kicking Horse and the warriors find evidence of a recent camp. The Chief turns to Catches Snake, "Tell us where they went?" The brave examines the tracks - then points West, "The Shoshone circle the Crow. Their fire is not old, we are not far behind." Kicking Horse turns to his warriors, "Soon, we will catch them - slay their braves and recapture the maidens." The Chetowa War Party sound out loud yells, whoops and war cries. The group ride out with great urgency.

* * *

Up ahead.

The Shoshone trek over some rugged terrain going slow, careful not to injure their horses' ankles. When the group reach rolling grasslands, they resume their regular pace as they ride over a seemingly endless expanse of grass. Two Knives scouts ahead and rides his horse to the top of a grassy elevation.

Running Dog and Catches Snake suddenly spot Two Knives on a distant ridge and alert the Chief, "They're up ahead! Kicking Horse and the Chetowa warriors spurn their mounts on with loud war cries!

Two Knives scans the direction from which they come - he's shocked! The Chetowa War Party ride toward them. Two Knives reins his horse around sprints down the slope to the others and cries, "The Chetowa are riding toward us!" Bear Claw yells out, "Everyone! Quick, ride! We must outrun them!" The alarmed Shoshone bolt their horses forward, the Shoshone ride hard eating up the ground.

The Chetowa chase the Shoshone across the plains. Bright Star, Willow and Singing Rain are afraid. Bear Claw, Thunder Cloud, Eagle Feather and Yuji ride beside them to encourage them on. Two Knives rides ahead and sees a grove of trees and brush to the left, he turns to Bear Claw and points and goes in that direction. The Shoshone steer their horses toward the cluster of trees. Riding into the grove, Bear Claw motions the group to stop. He sizes things up, "Take the maidens to the middle of the grove for safety. We will strike as they approach." He turns to his good friend Two Knives, "Ride to our people and get our warriors!" Two Knives nods and quickly races his mount through the trees and out the other side of the grove. Yuji comes beside Bear Claw, "The Shoshone Ninja and I will ambush them." Bear Claw nods agreement and the Shoshone braves take positions in the outer trees. Eagle Feather's group reach the middle of the grove - there's a clearing with a large pond of water. They dismount and tie the horses and ready their weapons. Eagle Feather steps over to Bright Star and the other maidens, "Take this rifle, these knives and tomahawks for defence." Bright Star grabs the rifle with resolve, "They will not take us without a fight!" The maidens grab weapons and stand ready. In the perimeter trees, the Shoshone hold their positions. The air fills with loud Chetowa war cries and battle screams. Bear Claw and the other braves watch from the woods.

The Chetowa thunder toward them - suddenly, Kicking Horse lifts up his lance and the riders stop. The war party halt a good distance out from the tree grove. The Shoshone look out at their pursuers - the Chetowa warriors poised for battle, their horses snort and paw the ground. Kicking Horse and the Chetowa observe the grove for movement within - nothing but an eerie stillness. Catches Snake remarks, "The Shoshone are hiding - waiting for us." The Chief ponders his warrior's words, then turns to a seasoned brave on his left and raises his lance, "Take a small group into the trees." The brave nods and waves those around him to ride forth. As the Chetowa riders approach the trees, the braves are met with rifle fire and arrows - most are killed except a few. The surviving Chetowa scurry back to rejoin the war party. Kicking Horse orders, "We will divide our braves and attack from two sides." The Chief signals and the Chetowa divide into two groups. Catches Snake leads a group to the left and Spotted Bird takes a group to attack the right. Within the trees, Bear Claw sees what the Chetowa are planning to do, "I will take braves to the left. Yuji - take your fighters to the right." Both Shoshone groups quickly disperse and rapidly run to their section of the trees. Outside the grove, the two Chetowa forces reach their position. Bear Claw and the Shoshone braves stand ready to stop Catches Snake and his group. On the opposite side of the trees, Yuji and the Shoshone Ninja are poised against Spotted Bird's warriors. Chief Kicking Horse and the remaining Chetowa warriors observe from a distance. The Chief lifts his spear and the two groups ride full force into the trees. As Catches Snake and his warriors ride into the grove, they are met with rifle fire, arrows and spears from Bear Claw and his braves. Yuji's fighters jump from trees, rocks and bushes to attack with swords, knives, metal stars and tomahawk - their Ninja skills have deadly accuracy. The two Chetowa groups suffer heavy casualty and retreat to rejoin Kicking Horse and the warriors. Catches Snake rides his horse up and the Chief notices the arrow in the braves's right thigh. Catches Snake grimaces and breaks off the arrow shaft, "The trees give them protection!" Kicking Horse studies the grove then turns to his warriors, "We will burn them out. Make ready your fire arrows!" Spotted Bird, Running Dog and others start small fires. The Chetowa warriors wrap grass and cloth strips around arrow heads, then dips them into the fire. With arrow ablaze, the Chetowa warriors tilt back, bend their bows and shoot flaming arrows into the trees. Bear Claw, Yuji and the others watch as flaming arrows land in the branches, trees and grass around them. With too many arrows to put out, Bear Claw, Yuji and the Shoshone braves run to the middle where Eagle Feather and the maidens are. They look around in all directions. Fire rages in the trees and grass, the flames moving toward them. Bear Claw and Thunder Cloud untie the horses to let the animals escape through the trees. Some braves show deep worry. Some maidens start to cry. Bear Claw is at his wits end as he sees walls of flame creeping toward them. Yuji looks at the pond and the reeds near the water's edge. He quickly runs over and pulls out a reed and cuts off both ends. All the Shoshone are puzzled by his action. Yuji looks at them, "Watch me and do the same!" Yuji jumps in and wades to the middle of the pond until he stands chest deep. He puts one end of the reed in his mouth and submerges and leaves the reed's open end above the water. A few seconds later he rises dripping wet. The Shoshone are stunned! Bear Claw is perceptive and yells, "Do like Yuji - cut reeds to stay under the water." Yuji lets everyone know, "Breathe through the reed. You can stay under the water and escape the fire!" As Yuji guides, the Shoshone swiftly cut reeds and enter the pond to the middle. They look around - the surrounding trees and grass are an inferno. At Yuji's signal they submerge under the water. A few braves and maidens swallow water - panic and stand. Yuji helps them to keep the reed at the right position to breathe. At last, all the Shoshone are under the water and safe! The fire burns the grove interior and everything is ablaze. Flames lick at the water's edge. The fire and smoke rise high in the air.

Kicking Horse and the Chetowa warriors watch the fire consume the grove, all the trees burning with fire, the flames shooting high in the air. When the fire dies down, all that remains are charred trees and scorched earth. Catches Snake, Running Dog and Spotted Bird ride up and are surprised to see no Shoshone - just blacken stumps and smouldering ground. The young tribe leader questions aloud, "Where did the Shoshone go" How did they escape?" The Chetowa warriors cannot believe their eyes and start to wonder aloud and murmur. Running Dog races his horse around the burnt grove and spots fresh horse tracks. He points, "Their horse tracks go this way!" Kicking Horse and the war party launch out in hot pursuit to follow Running Dog. The Chetowa war party disappear over the hill top.

A few moments pass…

Yuji lifts his head out of the water just enough to peer about. All around is burnt black with pockets of smouldering ground. Yuji taps Eagle Feather and Bear Claw to rise. The Shoshone braves and maidens stand up in the water and gaze around. The once green lush tree grove now nothing but black burnt ruins - and no Chetowa in sight. The group quickly stride out of the pond - everyone safe - everyone dripping wet. Bear Claw turns to his people, "We head for our Tribal lands on foot!" They all exchange quick glances and run out of the charred area and head south - toward home.

The Shoshone race across the grasslands. The pace is hectic, the braves assist whenever a maiden stumbles or falls down. The weary rescue party move at a steady rate going through the afternoon and into the evening. The sun sets and a full moon appears at night, its moonlight illuminates the ground. Bear Claw coaxes their travel through the night hours, and they take breaks whenever they get too tired.

As the sun rises, the braves and maidens walk in the early morning light. The group travel down the middle of a large grassy vale. All at once they hear yells, screams and war cries! The Shoshone turn about and see the Chetowa warriors off in the distance thundering toward them. The people look at Bear Claw, "We cannot outrun their horses. We make our stand here!" The Shoshone braves take forward positions to face the oncoming threat. The maidens move behind their warriors for protection. All the Shoshone stand ready with weapons in hand. Yuji glances at Bright Star, "Stay near me, I will protect you!" Bright Star grips Yuji's arm as the Chetowa warriors get closer and louder. Kicking Horse and Spotted Bird steer their horses to the side to stop and observe the battle. The encroaching first wave of Chetowa warriors let loose their arrows and spears. The Shoshone dodge and duck the barrage. Some arrows wound a couple of Shoshone braves. Oncoming Chetowa warriors ride up and leap from their horses and attack with tomahawks, knives and war clubs. The Shoshone Ninja repeal the assault - the fighting is intense. Yuji and the Shoshone Ninja use swords, tomahawks, chain darts and stars to cut down the attackers. The Chetowa are overpowered and destroyed by hand-to-hand combat. The Shoshone defeat all their attackers. They catch their breath and get ready for another assault! Kicking Horse is shocked and angry at the loss of so many of his warriors. He raises his Lance high before the large remaining group of Chetowa braves, "Kill them all - even the maidens! Avenge our fallen warriors!" The Chetowa begin to move in mass. Bear Claw, Eagle Feather, Yuji and the Shoshone brace for the impending doom. The Chetowa charge toward the small group.

Suddenly - Multiple Gun Shots!

The Shoshone and the Chetowa turn toward the gunfire. Chief Buffalo Sky, Two Knives and hundreds of Shoshone warriors ride over the hill crest. The Shoshone braves fill the air with loud war cries, yells and battle screams! The large Shoshone force descend the grassy slope toward Bear Claw and the others. Seeing the Shoshone warriors en masse, Kicking Horse, Spotted Bird and all the Chetowa braves turn around and flee. Spotted Bird insists to fight, "Father, the maidens are there. We are so close!" Kicking Horse looks at his young impetuous son, "We will not fight so many this far from home! - Quick! We return to our lands." The Chetowa war party bolt their horse and dash away putting distance between them and the big Shoshone war party. The small Shoshone rescue group break out in victory cheers! Buffalo Sky and the Shoshone braves ride up, and Bear Claw conveys his gratitude, "You brought our warriors in time!" The Chief replies, "Two Knives rode like the wind. His horse died after reaching camp. We knew you were in trouble." The Shoshone rescuers rejoice with big smiles, happy to be safe. The Shoshone braves hoist the rescuers atop their horses for the journey back to Shoshone lands. The massive Shoshone group head back home.

CHAPTER THIRTY-THREE
Yuji And Bright Star Are Married

It's a beautiful day with the sun shining in a clear blue sky. A gentle breeze flows through the trees and the meadows are filled with colourful wild flowers. Chief Buffalo Sky is in full regalia and feathered headdress. Eagle Feather wears a richly decorated tunic. The Shoshone Elders stand nearby. The entire village gather with happy faces and joyful expressions for the Wedding Ceremony. Yuji and Bright Star are getting married! Bright Star wears a soft white buckskin dress with exquisite beadwork and moccasins with fine embroidery and adorns herself with Yuji's beaded necklace. She looks like a beautiful Indian Princess! Yuji is dressed in a white kimono with detailed embroidery. He looks stately and handsome. The young couple stand before Eagle Feather and Buffalo Sky.

Eagle Feather lifts up his arm to the sky and chants a Shoshone prayer to the Great Spirit. Then he burns a bundled stalk of sweetgrass, sage and thyme - and waves the smoking bundle around the couple's heads, sides, front and back. Next, Eagle Feather joins the hands of Bright Star and Yuji together and wraps a sash of elaborate embroidery around the couple's hands, and speaks to them, "Your hands are joined together with the sacred cloth. Together in love! Together in life! - Bright Star, Yuji's tepee is now your tepee. He is your Dainah - you are his Wa'ipi! - Yuji, Bright Star is now yours to protect and care for! May your tepee be full of love, laughter, and little ones!" Eagle Feather tosses red powder in the air on all four sides of the couple. Next, he holds an eagle wing and passes it over the new husband and wife as he chants a Shoshone prayer. - Finished, Eagle Feather turns to Buffalo Sky. The Chief raises his arm and braves bring a stunning Appaloosa horse to him. The Chief passes the reins to Yuji, "We, the Shoshone people give you this handsome painted pony as a wedding gift!" Yuji bows respect. He and Bright Star stand with big smiles of joy and gratitude. The Chief lifts his hand, "Tonight, there will be a feast in honour of Yuji and Bright Star!" The villagers cheer in celebration.

As Bright Star and Yuji gaze around at the people sharing their happy occasion, Bear Claw, Thunder Cloud, Two Knives and Otter come up to the newly weds and lead the surprised couple away - the villagers follow. Bear Claw and the couple and the entourage merrily walk past many dwellings until they reach a newly constructed tepee. Bear Claw turns to Yuji and Bright Star, "The Shoshone braves and our Ninja warriors made this for your new home. Our wedding gift to you!" Yuji is humbled and bows to Bear Claw, the braves and the Ninja warriors. Bright Star's eyes sparkle as she views her new home. She's eager to enter and grabs Yuji's hand and pulls him to go inside. Bear Claw, the braves, the Shoshone Ninja, and the villagers laugh and chuckle at her excitement. Yuji looks at Bear Claw, "Bright Star wants me inside now - I must go." Bear Claw grins and jests, "The brave is the head, and the woman is the neck! Many times in life, you will find yourself being turned!" Yuji grins and waves to all as he and Bright Star enter their new home.

Two years later.

Outside his tepee, Yuji nervously paces back and forth. He stops, looks at the tepee, then begins to pace again. Eagle Feather, Bear Claw, Thunder Cloud, Two Knives and Otter grin and chuckle as they stand nearby. Yuji watches as old Shoshone women go in and out of the tepee. Yuji goes up beside the entrance to peer in and an old Shoshone woman shoes him away. He walks over to Eagle Feather, "I have faced battle - but I don't know if I'm ready for this!" Eagle Feather, his father-in-law, puts his hand on Yuji's shoulder, "You will do well." Loud cries and deep groans cause them to rivet attention at the tepee. They hear Bright Star strain - and then cry out - then silence. The men look at each other. Suddenly, the sound of a baby crying! Yuji's face lights up full of joy! He looks at the men close by and they all nod with happy smiles. The tepee flap lifts open and an old Shoshone woman waves Yuji to come inside now. Yuji enters the tepee and pauses. Bright Star is on a platform of fur robes - she's exhausted and perspiring, yet she beams with pure joy. The young mother holds her new baby! Yuji comes over and kneels beside mother and baby. Yuji is in awe! Bright

Star smiles and lifts her hand to touch Yuji, "You have a son!" Yuji reaches out and tenderly lifts up his newborn and gazes at him with wonder and deep joy, "A son! I have a son!" Bright Star looks up at Yuji and baby, "What name will you give him?" Yuji softly gazes at the tiny infant in his arms, he looks at Bright Star, then looks again at the baby, "I name him - Kamatsu! It means victorious son." Bright Star replies with a sweet expression, "It is a good name!" Yuji lovingly holds the baby that's wrapped in a soft blanket and carefully exits the tepee. He carries the newborn to Eagle Feather, Bear Claw, Thunder Cloud, Two Knives and Otter to see. Yuji announces, "Bright Star and I have a son! A healthy baby boy!" The men tenderly gaze at the baby and wide smiles break out. Yuji proudly carries his newborn son back inside the tepee.

Kamatsu grows to become an adorable two year old with bright dark eyes and a cute smile to melt the heart. One afternoon, Yuji and Kamatsu are in the forest to enjoy nature. Yuji laughs as little Kamatsu chases after fluttering butterflies. In the meadow, Yuji points and shows his son a chipmunk. The little boy is so intrigued as he holds a beautiful flower in his tiny fingers. Father and son watch a bird chirp as it sits on a tree branch. Yuji shows Kamatsu some baby bunnies - it's pure fascination for the tiny tot. In the grassy meadow, Kamatsu giggles as he chases Yuji. And when Yuji chases, Kamatsu giggles some more. An afternoon of play is hard work, and the father and son take a break. Yuji lays on his back in the meadow, and the son sits on dad's tummy being playful. Suddenly, Kamatsu becomes frozen - his eyes stare ahead. Yuji notices his son's stillness and with a hand on Kamatsu, he rolls over and stands to his feet. Not far away is a large black timber wolf. Instinctively, Yuji steps in front of Kamatsu to shield and protect him. He keeps one arm on the boy. Yuji reaches behind to grab his short Ninjato sword still in the scabbard. Yuji brings the sword in front to be ready. Surprised! Alarmed! Yuji scans the forest - there are no other wolves. Yuji and the big wolf lock eyes! Yuji can hear the sound of his own heartbeat quicken. Thump! Thump! Thump! Yuji and the big timber wolf lock eyes for the longest time. Then, the large animal suddenly turns and swiftly disappears into the forest. Yuji sighs relief and looks down at tiny Kamatsu who has a big smile. Yuji lifts his son onto his shoulders and heads home. As Yuji and Kamatsu enter the family tepee, Bright Star greets them with a loving smile.

CHAPTER THIRTY-FOUR
The Ninjans and Cutter's Demise

High up in the rugged mountains, Shoshone hunters and trappers trek through the forest trail, their horses laden heavy with animal furs. The quietness is shattered with gunshots from rifles and pistols. The Shoshone braves are shot off their horses and hit the ground. One brave, wounded in the shoulder, gets up and runs to escape. Bullets whiz around him but he disappears into the dense brush. Cutter and a large group of bandits emerge from hiding. The outlaws rush in to grab the horses and furs, then rob and scalp the dead Indians. The outlaws revel in the excitement. Cutter barks at his men, "Make sure those Indians are dead!" Cutter and his gang lead the fur ladened horses up the forest trail to an old abandoned mining camp. The camp has four wood buildings, Cutter and the outlaws use the large wood building as their hideout. The bandits offload the horses and store the furs inside their quarters. The afternoon sun sets and night takes over.

A day and a half pass.

Inside the large wood bunkhouse, Cutter and his men relax and gloat over their stolen bounty of horses, furs, gold and scalps. Some men drink Whiskey while other smoke cigarettes and play cards. Some are sprawled out asleep or just rest. A few clean their pistols and rifles. On the front porch outside, a bandit hangs the Shoshone scalps on a line to dry. Whoosh! Whoosh! A black arrow pierces deep into the outlaw's shoulder. In great pain, he stumbles inside shouting, "Indians! We're surrounded by Indians!" Cutter and the men grab their guns and race to the door and windows. They break the glass and aim their pistols and rifles. Whoosh! Whoosh! Black arrows rain down on the dry wood structure - hitting the door, walls and windows. Cutter and the bandits fire their guns. There's a momentary lull. Then -

repeated thuds! Burning arrows strike the door, porch, roof and walls. Flames start to spread across the dry wood building - the large cabin quickly catches fire and smoke begins to fill the room. Cutter hunkered down at a window, coughs and bellows, "Shoot your way out - Kill 'em all!"

The outlaws pour out of the hideout with guns blazing! Cutter and the outlaws try to scatter. Many are killed by sword, tomahawk, arrows and sharp metal stars. As others are being decimated, Cutter manages to reach the barn where two braves attack him. He gets sliced deep from the sword and shot with an arrow, but he manages to shoot the attackers. He's greatly wounded and stumbles to a large tree where he slumps down against the trunk. He grimaces in pain! Cutter lifts up his eyes to see dark figures coming toward him. He points his gun. Click! Click! Empty! Cutter leans back against the trunk and grabs his side as blood gushes out to form a small pool. He watches the figures dressed in black get close. Their outfits - a blend of Indian and Ninja. Each warrior wears fierce war paint and bristles with deadly weapons - swords, tomahawk, knife, war club, bow and arrows. The leader comes up and stands before Cutter - it's Otter! Cutter looks at Otter from head to foot and smirks, "Indians." Otter bends down and looks Cutter straight in the eye and firmly replies, "Ninjans! - We are Ninjans!"

In the mountain forest, a pack of timber wolves sniff the air, the fresh scent of blood alert their appetite. Howls erupt! The wolf pack start to run. The wolf howls carry to the mining camp. Cutter turns his head to the woods, then back toward Otter and frantically pleads, "You can't leave me like this! - Not like this! Give me some bullets. Some ammo!" Otter and the other Ninjans watch stone-faced, then turn and walk away and disappear into the forest. Cutter is gripped with raw fear! He glances about every which way. The wolf pack run past the big building littered with dead outlaws, and make straight for the wounded bleeding man. Cutter watches as the wolf pack surround him - snarling and growling. The wolves bare their sharp fangs and snap their jaws. Cutter looks in front as the big Alpha wolf creeps closer and closer, the animal's saliva drips from its open jaw and sharp teeth. Cutter grabs the pistol with his trembling hand to use it as a club. The big wolf lets out a vicious snarl - then leaps!

THE END